Getting Away With Murder

AILEEN PLUKER

ACKNOWLEDGEMENTS

Thanks to Rosemary and Mary
for proofreading and publishing assistance.

Other Books by Aileen Pluker

My Name Is SOS

Margaret Catchpole

Tammie

If Only

CHAPTER 1

ADELAIDE – 2008

In Adelaide the best people live in the middle. The wealthy might build their glass mansions by the sea, intellectuals and alternatives, their pine wood, eco-friendly lodges in the hills, but those who matter, the 'old money', live in solid, limestone, nineteenth century houses, built with care, designed to last, set in well-tended English gardens. They were built in a time when servants were a given and spacious enough for family gatherings when country cousins came to visit.

We come from 'old money', as my grandmother, Flora Henderson-Mudge, constantly reminds me. When she married she inherited such a house. She named it Glencoe, in honour of her forebears who were betrayed by the Campbells and suffered and died in that infamous massacre of long ago.

I, Sally Richards, am the youngest surviving member of this branch of the illustrious clan and I am never allowed to forget it. The wealth may have diminished, the obligations haven't. We are civilized people and are expected to set an example to those less well bred. Grandmother's fortune and our reputation were made in Queensland, but that matters little because the squattocracy is a clan without borders and our clan, the MacEanruig, already had an illustrious history in Scotland long before Australia existed.

The Mudges, though not so illustrious, come from a long line of academics.

Alexandra Ladies Academy called after Queen Alexandra, she of the choker necklaces and the upswept curls, was founded at the beginning of the twentieth century, by two formidable women. It was dedicated to the education and advancement of young girls, intelligent of mind and temperate in attitude, committed to the preservation of British, Christian values. It is fighting a losing battle in this century but still strives to turn out fine examples of what society sees as exemplary women. Of course Q. A., who still looks down on us each morning from her portrait in the assembly hall, is to be our example - her charitable works - her devotion to family and country and her progressive feminine attitude. She even had swimming lessons!!! Nothing is ever mentioned about putting up with a promiscuous husband. We only found out about that from reading history books not on the syllabus.

I am the third generation of Henderson lineage to grace this establishment. Grandmother Flora attended, not as a pupil, but as a teacher, a subject not often mentioned, but explained by a temporary financial setback, caused when a 'dastardly relative' did her out of her inheritance in Queensland. She removed herself from that state to earn her living in South Australia as a French and Latin teacher.

This blip was temporary as she soon snared the honourable Archibald Mudge, professor at the Adelaide University and grandson of a British Peer.

He was quite a dear, Grandy Archy, a little eccentric, but he filled my childhood with endless tales of wonder and adventure.

It was a pity he died when I was ten.

My mother takes after him. My life could have been one of comfortable happiness had not my father, Geoffrey Richards, who caught a nasty virus while defending the rights of the oppressed, died when I was four. Mother, who had no income, had to move back to Glencoe, a lovely sandstone building that passes for our ancestral home. From then I was raised under the iron rule of Grandmother Flora Henderson-Mudge.

My mother had been a great disappointment to Flora, didn't finish her degree and became caught up in peace movements, inspired by the students in the Tiananmen Square Massacre. She and my dad left their studies and spent the next few years joining one protest group after another. It must have been a wonderful life, if one was young and didn't mind living in poverty.

Mother must have lost her rebellious streak after my father's death and, having grown up under her mother's discipline, slipped back into old ways, believing that acquiescence was the best way to survive.

Grandmother is determined that I will not make the same mistake but instead, do credit to my bloodline. So, though it is now the twenty first century, I still live a way of life not unlike that of the nineteenth.

When it all get too much for me, Mum consoles me with the thought that once I get away to university, hopefully in another state, I will be able to live a life of my own, like she did. I hope she's right.

I have managed to survive seventeen summers without blotting my copybook so the end is in sight. Only two obstacles stand in my way. First, good matric. marks, which I am determined to get even if I go blind in the process, and second, finding the right partner for the Formal, an archaic practice which once signified a young person was ready to join society. Mum said that in her day it was called "making one's debut" and really meant something. Now it is just an excuse for a dress-up that happens in one's final year at school.

The dress, the necklace, the hairstyle have all been chosen. All I need now is a suitable partner. Any prospective young man has to pass the scrutiny of the Formidable Flora. This is done by inviting one or two suitables home for a social evening.

Anyone would think I had the pick of dozens of eligibles, but my life has been so controlled that I have few male acquaintances apart from brothers of friends. The only ones I am remotely interested in have already been well and truly snared. The rest are a pretty boring lot.

But a week or so ago, I met a friend of a friend who might fit the bill. I have made discrete enquiries and he seem eminently suitable, family-wise, and in the couple of conversations I have had with him, seems able to hold his own. Whether he can dance or not is beside the point.

Of course he knows the score. We all do. It's part of the ritual and most times is reciprocated when their Formal comes around. Oh. It's a great social whirl in Adelaide when the end of school is nigh. Fanny Mae and Freddie Mac may have caused disaster on the stock exchange but in little old Adelaide we have our priorities right. The world might be "going to hell in a hand basket" but here it's "Formals before the Fall."

CHAPTER 2

Among our crowd it is a custom to have informal dinner parties from time to time. It is a way of catching up outside of school hours, and of introducing new friends to the group to see if they are acceptable. You can tell a lot about a person over dinner.

But this time I had a vested interest. I was introducing Joel Forbes, my prospective partner, not to my friends who already knew him, but to the family, especially the matriarch Flora, for a tick of approval.

Mum had been watching the weather all day. Spring is a trick season in Adelaide especially early in September. She decided we could risk drinks outside.

In the grounds of Glencoe we have an outdoor structure, called, would you believe it, *The Pavilion*!!! It consists of a large cement slab with rather nice stone pillars and a tiled roof. It really is quite a nice place on a balmy evening, but a "pavilion"?

A group of my friends, male and female, were enjoying pre-dinner drinks there, non-alcoholic except for the punch, which was by far the favourite, when Grandmother made her entrance. Though no longer the 'great beauty' she assures us she had been, she still has a presence. Two of my girlfriends and their brothers, whom she had already met, were acknowledged, before she waited for me to introduce the remaining guests.

'This is Grace Hamilton, Grandmother. Grace this is my Grandmother Flora Henderson-Mudge.'

Grandmother extended her hand. 'A pleasure to meet you, Grace.'

'Grace is a relative of your friend, Mrs Toft.'

Grandmother bestowed a smile on her. 'And what is your relationship with Vivien?'

'She is my Great Aunt.' Grace was still holding the hand, not quite knowing what to do with it.

'You must give her my best regards.' Grandmother withdrew the hand and a nod signified that Lucy's pedigree made her acceptable.

'And this is Joel.' I was so nervous that I mucked up the introduction.

Poor Joel stepped forward but, instead of extending her hand, Grandmother gave a slight frown. Had it been another era I'm sure she would have raised her lorgnette but had to do with a raised eyebrow.

'Joel whom?' she enquired.

'Sorry, Grandmother.' I had so wanted to make a good impression and I'd blown it. Joel just stood there like an actor waiting in the wings for his cue. I tried again. 'Grandmother, this is Joel Forbes. He is . . .' My voice faltered. Grandmother's lips had tightened. There was coldness in her eyes. I tried again.

'He is the son of the gentleman who was recently elected to the Upper House.' I said all this in a rush but I could see she was not listening.

'Forbes? Did you say Forbes?' Then to Joel, 'Has your family always lived in South Australia?'

'For three generations, yes Ma'am, but originally we came

from Queensland, Brisbane actually.'

I was proud of him, holding his own against that withering stare. I was a bit taken aback by the 'ma'am' but was sure it would win him brownie points. However Grandmother did not so much as acknowledge him. Even though he had never met her before, he must have recognized the chill.

Instead she turned to my mother, 'Lavinia, you will have to excuse me from dinner. I will have a small plate in my room.'

'Are you unwell, Mother?'

The receding figure answered the question with a dismissive gesture and continued regally towards her part of the house.

'Well, I wonder what has got into her?' Mum said, giving Joel a weak smile, then raising her voice slightly to be heard above the chatter, 'When you have finished your drinks, entrée will be served in the dining room.'

We trooped in behind her and the evening turned out to be a success after all. Grandmother's absence certainly made it a more relaxed affair.

By the end of the evening I'd decided that I really liked Joel, as a person, not just as a dancing partner. I popped the question and he said 'yes'. We were getting on like a house on fire and I didn't object when his parting kiss on the cheek was pretty close to my mouth.

I was feeling pleased with myself as I walked back into the house, but was surprised by Grandmother, who materialized beside me and grabbed my arm.

'Don't you ever let that young man into this house again,' she hissed, then moved back towards her quarters.

I was shocked. Joel came from a good family and, during the few minutes she had observed him, had behaved like a perfect gentleman. What did Grandmother have against him, apart from the fact he came from Queensland? She couldn't condemn him for that? Surely she didn't have an objection to the entire state? Or, could he be a descendant of the 'dastardly relative' who had 'done her in'?

I knew I would not get an explanation from her, but I wanted answers. I liked the guy. In fact I was becoming fonder of him by the minute and, more importantly, I had asked him to partner me. I wasn't going to give him up without a very good reason.

As I helped Mum pack the dishwasher I asked, 'Mum, you know the dastardly relative who robbed Grandmother, his name wasn't Forbes, by any chance?'

'No. He was a Henderson, her uncle, if I remember. Why?'

'Well, she took an instant dislike to Joel. As soon as she heard his name she just gave him that icy stare she gives when someone has upset her.'

'What a pity, and I thought he was such a nice boy. Oh, well we will just have to keep on looking until we find one that suits her.'

That was mum, peace at any price.

'Yeah. I can imagine what he'll be like. No, I'm sick of this Mum. Someone has got to stand up to her.'

'I know darling, but she's been calling the shots for so long I doubt anyone could stop her now. Don't give in and antagonise her when the end is so near. When you go to Uni, in Melbourne perhaps, or even Perth, she will not be able to do anything about it. It worked for me. It will work for you too. Just have a bit more patience.'

But I'm not going to give in so easily. Unless I am given a very good reason why not, Joel is going to be my partner or I won't go to the Formal at all, even if it meant being chopped off the family tree, thrown on the streets and forced to fend for myself.

Who did these Henderson's think they were anyway?

19th Century

Ewan Henderson, a poor descendant of the ancient clan MacEanruig, left his beloved Scotland in 1843 with an abiding hatred of the Sassenach and a determination to re-establish the honour and fortune of his ancestors in the new world.

He worked on a sheep station in Victoria for two years, but as the best of the spreads had already been taken, he headed north to Moreton Bay where pastures were there for the taking.

Though he lived with a burning grievance for the robbing of his ancestral land, he had no qualms in taking possession of land that had belonged to another race for millennia.

In time his land grab was legalised and he became a wealthy pastoralist, his property extending far beyond his wildest dreams. He was ready to establish his own dynasty. At his head station he built a substantial homestead from local timbers with spacious verandas, which he called Lochaber. He sent for his sweetheart who, as a thirteen year old, had promised to wait for him.

Twenty five year old Jeanie had kept her promise.

Throughout the long sea voyage to Australia and the subsequent journey to remote Brisbane she never lost her faith that Ewan would be waiting. They were married in Brisbane.

Two days later they set out for her new home.

Jeannie presented him with two strong sons and a delicate daughter Ebilin. The children were home schooled by their mother until the boys were old enough to become boarders at Brisbane Grammar School. There they were educated to become members of the pastoral gentry of this strange, new land.

To crown his achievements Ewan acquired a few acres in the newly formed suburb of New Farm and built a large two storey house, in the Georgian style, with sixteen rooms, a detached kitchen with covered walkway, a great hall and a central staircase made from local cedar of which he was particularly proud.

The move to Brisbane had been necessary, as Ebilin, never robust, became seriously ill and needed constant nursing and proximity to reliable medical care. Her health had been the impetus to build *Inverrigan*. Jeanie took up residence there and Ewan moved between the stations and Brisbane until the boys were old enough to take over. He had trained his sons well and was confident that they could manage, though no purchase or decision was taken without his approval.

In Brisbane he became active in civic duties and represented the pastoralists in parliament.

In time, Ewan's body, worn down by years of toil began to betray him. Soon Jeanie was nurse to two ailing people. As she sat, through the night, keeping vigil over father and daughter she wondered who would be first to go. Ebilin won the deadly race but her father joined her in less than a year. It was then that Jeanie's robust constitution began to fail. She lingered on for a number of years but was never the mistress she had hoped to be when they had first moved to *Inverrigan*.

CHAPTER 3

ADELAIDE

Before school next day I rang Joel. I wanted to discuss my problem face to face so asked if he would meet me after school at the Pigs in the Mall. When I arrived he was already there, looking rather anxious. We went to Coffee House and found an empty table.

We both began to speak at once then Joel, always the gentleman, said, 'You go first.'

I took a deep breath. How was I going to broach this subject?

'Well, you have met my grandmother.'

'And she didn't like me.'

'No. . er . .yes, but it doesn't mean anything. Sometimes she's like that. Takes a set against someone for no good reason.'

'Oh, there's a good reason all right.'

Great, Joel had the answer to my quandary. 'There is? What is it?'

'Now there's the problem. I was hoping that you could tell me.'

What a disappointment. 'Well, I don't know what it is either. As soon as I mentioned your surname . . .'

'Same here. When I got home Dad asked me how the dinner went, who was there, you know, just making conversation. But the minute I mentioned your grandmother's name his expression changed. "Did you say Flora Henderson?" and I said 'Yes. Flora Henderson-Mudge. Do you know her?'

'And?'

'And he said, "No, but I've heard of her, I don't think you should visit that house again." And even though I pestered him he wouldn't say any more, except that it was old history and best left alone.'

We looked at each other and laughed. Then his expression changed 'So, I suppose the Formal's off?'

'No Joel, I still want you to be my partner, now more than ever. But what about your Dad?'

'Oh, he'll go along with it. It's your grandmother who seems to be the problem.'

You can say that again. When Fearsome Flora assumes a position it takes a bomb to move her. We had a problem, but it was mine to solve.

'Well I don't care. I've lived by her rules all my life. If you still want to, be my partner I mean, I'm going to make a stand. Either someone tells me what the problem is or they can all go hang.'

'Funny you should say that, because I think this all has to do with a hanging, or a murder, at least.'

'A murder!' Suddenly this feud was getting interesting. 'What happened?'

'Again, I don't know, but I remember Grandad talking about something that happened years ago in Brisbane. It was why he left Queensland.'

'Wow, this is unbelievable. A secret murder in the family. I've never heard anything about that. I'll ask Mum, but, as usual, she will probably know nothing about it. You better get the story from your grandad.'

'I can't. He's been dead for eight years. Dad's a bit like your Mum, see no evil think no evil. The only clue I have is that when Grandad was getting a bit senile he kept saying, over and over, "I blamed him for the murder and he was innocent all the time." It seemed to play on his mind.'

Once again, just as this story was getting interesting, I was faced with a blank.

'Then we'll have to find out for ourselves.'

'I've always fancied myself as Sherlock Holms.' He held up an imaginary magnifying glass.

'So, I suppose I'm Dr Watson?'

Joel nodded. 'I'll try to find out all I can on my side, see if I can find the connection to yours.'

'I'll do the same and I think I will start with the revered Douglas Henderson. It couldn't go back any further than him surely?'

'I wouldn't be surprised, but we've got to start somewhere. I take it I'm still the chosen one?'

'You bet. We've got six weeks to solve this problem or else we will both defy our parents and go to the ball together in spite of them.'

'Sounds like the end of a fairy tale.'

'Or the beginning of a grand romance'

I think I blushed. I could hardly believe I had said that.

'I'll drink to that'

We raised out lattes in a toast and grinned at each other.

I was beginning to like him more and more.

Well, if I thought I had problems before I didn't know the half of it. A murder in the family!!! But who and why? And what did it have to do with the Henderson's and the Forbes'?

And, as if that wasn't enough, I think I'm falling for the guy. I say 'think' because, even though I'm very good at handing out free advice to my friends about their love life, when it comes to my own, I know less than nothing. I've been too busy working on the grand escape plan to get emotionally involved with anyone. The plan was to wait till I got to Uni. to do that.

I think I need a bit of advice myself, but I'm too embarrassed to ask any of my friends. I've always presented myself as the authority on things of the heart. I've read all the books but they don't help much, either. Good on the nuts and bolts but not so strong on the oils that moves them.

I wasted good sleeping hours worrying about this new problem, *feeling*? so decided to talk it over with my mother. She's the great romantic.

'Mum, when you first went to Melbourne Uni., before you met Dad, I mean, did you party all night and have lots of boyfriends?'

'Heavens no. It was the time of the Grim Reaper.'

'The what?'

'The Grim Reaper. It was a very effective campaign about A.I.D.S.'

'A.I.D.S.?'

'Yes. It may sound silly now but then it certainly put the brakes on our sex life. The sexual revolution of the 70s was in full swing when the epidemic broke out. At first it seemed to be confined to the homosexual population so we weren't so worried but by 1984 we knew that anyone could contract it. We didn't know all that much about it except that it was sexually transmitted and there was no cure. We were so afraid that we almost demanded a medical certificate before we would hold hands.'

'So, no partying around?'

'Oh yes. We still did that. You can't keep romance down, but we were careful and certainly not promiscuous.'

'So Dad was your only boyfriend?'

'Not quite, but as soon as I met him I knew he was the one.'

She was getting all misty and I hadn't even asked my question yet. 'But how did you know?'

'I can't explain darling, but when it happens to you, you will know too?'

Well, that was a help. I could have got more information from a trashy magazine. Still I could see she was trying.

'Thanks Mum.'

'Was there a special reason for asking?'

I could see that look in her eye. My mother is the original romantic. She would like nothing better than to believe I too had found my soul mate. If I announced I was going to elope I think she would have helped me pack.

'No special reason. I was just hoping that there might be more to University than study. I've been doing that all my life.'

'Oh, but there is Sally. Just wait until you get there. That's when you begin to live.'

CHAPTER 4

Well, that little talk was a big help!!! I think I'll try to put my feelings for Joel on the back burner and concentrate on the family mystery.

I now have three problems, well really two problems and a challenge. I have to find out what the bad blood is between the Henderson's and the Forbes'. I hope it doesn't go back to bonny Scotland and all the fighting between the Jacobites and William of Orange, though it wouldn't surprise me.

It's stupid. A month ago I didn't know a feud even existed and now it's coming between me, and my choice of a partner for the most important event in my limited social life. But I'm not going to give in that easily. I may not look like a Henderson but I think I have inherited some of their fighting spirit. I want Joel for my partner.

Truth to tell, the partner thing is just an excuse now. I like the guy. I really like the guy. Who knows, he might be the One. But that's getting a bit ahead of myself. The way I see it, I have a long, long way to go and many places to see before I think the big M word. But there's nothing to say that I can't take a buddy along as well.

Back to the present; the family secret, a possible murder and two ancient men. I do hope there's a murder. Joel's job is to find out all he can about that. Mine's to put old Douglas Henderson under the microscope. His name has hovered over me for as long as I can remember but I really know little about him apart from the fact that the family wealth disappeared under his watch.

There's a large picture of him in what Grandmother likes to call, the reception room! As if we were an hotel or something. He's up there on the wall so you can't miss him as you enter – a head and shoulders shot. He is young, dark haired, big, black moustache, waxed at the ends, heavy eyebrows and dark, steely eyes.

In fairness, it is a handsome face but I can't see any warmth in it. But then you never see smiling pictures of men from those days. Life must have been pretty serious. As a child I was afraid to come in here. I was sure he was watching me and finding fault with my very existence. I was definitely not a Henderson.

Still, there must have been some love in him. Grandmother adored him and often tells stories of the adventures they had together. And he never married again, so he must have loved his wife.

I've just realised I have no idea what my Great Grandmother looks like. There's not one photo, not even a wedding photo. Strange that. They used to be big on wedding photos in those days. Another thought – I don't even know her name. Mum is called after Grandi's mother. Perhaps the second name, Elizabeth, is after her grandmother.

All this mystery is doing my brain in and I have to take care of it, as it is my ticket out of here. I wish I could get Grandmother to just accept Joel. Then I could leave all the sleuthing till matric. is over. Instead I have to waste precious study time getting the low down on my Great Grandfather Douglas Henderson.

Mum never knew him so I will have to try my investigating skills on dear old Flora.

Later in the day I decided to ask the font of knowledge of all things Henderson.

'Grandmother, how old was Great Grandfather when that picture in the reception room was taken?'

I knew that Flora was always more than willing to speak about her father. Perhaps she might say something interesting that would give me a lead.

'I am not sure Sally. It must have been done long before I was born. It was painted when he was a young man. I can always remember it over the mantle in the main hall. It was one of the few things I brought with me when I came south.'

'Was that in the big house?' I knew with the mention of *Inverrigan* she would start to go on about the history of the Hendersons, the MacEanruigs and the story of the Highland clearings but I hoped that, in doing so, she might say something interesting that would help me with my search. I listened patiently, for once, but she didn't drop one detail that I had not heard before, over and over. I've heard about the treacherous deeds of the Campbells so often that I have an unconscious suspicion of all those who bear the name.

'Why did you have to leave *Inverrigan*, Grandmother? After all it was your father's house.'

'It has always been so among the Hendersons. Only eldest sons can inherit. I was a woman so I did not count.'

I could see the anger still burning in those old eyes. I felt, perhaps for the first time, a moments sorrow for her. What kind of woman would she have been if things had been different?

'Why didn't Great Grandfather marry again so that he could have a son?'

'Loyalty and love, my dear. Something your generation knows little about, especially loyalty.'

'He really must have loved his wife. What was her name, Grandmother? Is Mum called after her?'

An innocent question but I could see the reaction, the sudden coldness, like a blast of freezing air. She had shut down again, but she left with one passing shot. 'Your mother was named after her maternal grandmother.'

I already knew that. Mum hated it and was Livvy to all her friends. It was the second name, Elizabeth, that I was interested in. But I didn't get a chance to ask. The ice wall had descended. Why should the mention of her mother's name upset her so? If I were grieving for my mother I would want my grandchildren to know all about her. Surely part of loving someone is to keep their memory alive. But I suppose that would stir emotions and Flora does not do emotion.

This feud must have begun in Australia. Perhaps the dastardly relies were involved, but I didn't want to get into a discussion about them too. I hope Joel is having better luck.

But it got me thinking about the man in the picture. Would I have liked Douglas Henderson?

CHAPTER 5

BRISBANE - 1938

Douglas Henderson was a handsome man, a shade under six-foot, broad shoulders, a full head of black hair and blue green eyes that could turn to ice when defied but glinted like sun on sea when he smiled. He felt himself a worthy descendant of the great MacDonald clan.

He stood on the front step, whisky in hand, surveying his kingdom. It was lucky that May had been born in the month for which she was named, he thought. Spring and Summer were often problematic when planning outdoor activities in Brisbane but the month of May was always warm without being oppressive and tropical storms had passed.

The grounds of *Inverrigan* were at their best. A mixture of tropical and English trees and flowers, it was one of the premier gardens of the north. His mother, Jeanie, had devoted the latter years of her life to planning and planting it. She would have approved of his stewardship. As she would of the groups of young people sitting in groups talking, walking in twos and threes around the gardens or watching a game of tennis on the court at the side of the house.

He liked watching young people, especially young girls on the cusp of womanhood, ripening apples with the first blush of red speaking of the sweet juices inside, and he would have liked to be the one who took the first bite.

He had done plenty of that in his youth. In fact it had been just such an indulgence in Cairo in 1915 that had nearly cost him his life. By a strange turn of events it had also probable saved it. He was too ill to join his best mate, Darby Swann, in the hellhole called Gallipoli.

Instead when he recovered he became part of the 1st Imperial Camel Corps, suppressing the Senussi. He remained in Egypt until the end of hostilities. He knew that the campaigns he had been involved in had played as big a part in defending the Empire but they had not got the publicity of other campaigns and it was not the kind of war he had expected to be part of when he had joined up in Australia. He was restless so, instead of returning home when peace was declared, he spent some time in Southern Africa.

Darby had survived but, ruined in health, had been among the first of the wounded to be repatriated to Australia. He survived only long enough to marry Jessica Farrell and sire the beautiful May.

Douglas himself had only been saved from matrimony because of the ire of a Boer father who had never forgiven the British for taking his land. In his idle moments Douglas sometimes wondered if some seed of his was now growing to manhood on the Veldt.

He had been summoned home when his father's death was imminent and was in time to receive his father's blessing along with instructions of how he was to protect and increase the family holdings. Being the elder son, he inherited the responsibility for the Henderson empire. He took up residence at *Inverrigan* and, like his father, divided his time between Brisbane and the Lochaber stations.

When he had first returned to Australia he had had little interest in matrimony, but now he was getting on. Forty-one was a good time to get down to the business of extending his lineage. He certainly didn't want his little brother Charles and his tribe to inherit the family wealth.

He watched, as Jessica Swann moved from group to group like the good hostess she was. He had taken her and her daughter into his household after Darby died, to be housekeeper and companion for the ailing Jeannie. For a time, he knew she had had hopes of becoming his wife but he had been too restless to settle and later she no longer appealed to him. He wanted young blood to stir his loins and he had watched it, as it grew before his eyes.

At first he had felt nothing but a protective, fatherly love for the little orphaned daughter of his best friend. But as she grew in charm and beauty it had turned to desire. The last two years had been agony.

He had waited long enough. Today they were celebrating her eighteenth birthday. The next celebration would be her marriage.

May, unaware of her guardian's plans for her, was indulging in her favourite pastime, flirting. Her latest victim was a shy young man, William Forbes, who worked for Driver and Hoe, the leading architectural firm in Brisbane.

He did not belong to any of the prominent families and

couldn't believe his luck when the beautiful May Swann began singling him out for special attention. He was in love with her and believed she shared his feelings. William felt that life could never be more sweet.

"She loves me," sang his heart as he watched May, laughing and sharing little confidences with her two best friends. She is probably telling them about her party dress, he thought, proud of her talents. She had designed it herself. Or, perhaps she is telling them about us. I don't mind if she does. I want to shout it from the rooftops. But she has sworn me to secrecy.

Both Darby and Jessica had been good looking and the best of both their features had been reproduced in May. She had her mother's faultless English skin and big, blue eyes and Darcy's golden curls and generous mouth. When May smiled, Jessica always felt a stab of pain as she recognised the cheeky grin that had first attracted her to him.

It had been her smile that had first caught William Forbes' eye too but it was May herself who had won his heart. She was the most popular girl in the crowd of which they were a part and she could have had any one of the eligible young bachelors, most of them from the wealthy families of Queensland. But she had chosen him. Of course it had to be kept secret until he had established himself.

'I do love you Willie,' She had said. 'I really do and I do want to marry you, but you will have to make a name for yourself first. Dear Uncle Douglas would be terribly upset if I married someone with no money at all.'

'But I will make pots of money when I'm through my papers.'

'I know. But that is the future and what would we live on in the meantime? I do not want to sound like a spoilt child, but I really could not live in a hut. We will just have to wait.'

He didn't mind. He wanted to give her everything. He would wait forever for her. But would she?

'May, you know I will never love anyone but you. I can wait, but what if some wealthy suitor gets in before me?'

'Willie,' she pouted, 'do you not trust me. I believe you do not love me at all.'

'I do. I do. But I am jealous of every chap who so much as looks at you.'

'Silly. Do you have such little faith in me? Now give me a kiss ... not like that, everyone will see us, just a little kiss on the cheek.'

She had turned her head sideways and he obliged. She turned full face, gave him a promising wink then had skipped off to join her friends.

Willie wanted to pinch himself. His life was like a fairy tale, plucked from obscurity to be turned into the lucky prince who won the maiden's hand. Only, in his case there had been no magic, just a bit of luck and a lot of hard work.

Orphaned at an early age he was destined for a life of grinding poverty in Glasgow, but an uncle, in far away Australia, on a visit home to Bonny Scotland, had heard of his plight, saw intelligence in his clear blue eyes and taken him back as a kind of souvenir.

His early learning had been brief, but a couple of years with a private tutor and a determination to prove his worth to his uncle had seen him succeed and to eventually gain an apprenticeship with Driver and Hoe. One more year, and he would be fully qualified. He had already been offered a place in the firm, but his dream was to one day have his own business and to design and build beautiful buildings for the growing city.

And now, the most wonderful girl in all the world had promised to wait for him. What more incentive did he need?

Willie felt a playful punch on the shoulder. 'Reckon you're in with a chance there.'

Gerard Reid! Willie was tempted to punch him back, and not a friendly punch either. Where had he come from, what had he heard and, more importantly, why was he snooping around?

Willie, ignoring him, walked away, his balloon of happiness burst. He seriously didn't like Gerard but was not going to get into a fight with him

CHAPTER 6

Douglas caught Jessica's eye. 'Jess, leave the young things to look after themselves for a while. I have a matter to discuss with you.'

She was reluctant to leave the happy groups. Their carefree chatter made her feel young again. Her own youth had been too brief. She had once been the toast of the town, could have had her pick from all the eligible young men, but the Great War cut a swathe through their ranks. Out of a mixture of pity and patriot zeal she had chosen poor, ailing, shell-shocked Darby Swann.

That had been the end of her happy future.

Between illness and night terrors, her role became nurse and keeper. Socialising was no more. She rose each day, fearful of what it would bring, thankful if the night had been a peaceful one. There must have been some love, some tender moments but they were long forgotten in the constant nightmare of living with Darby.

The one consolation was May. Looking back she wondered how the girl had been conceived at all. But she had, and she was the one blessing, the golden gift for her years of sacrifice. However, their early days had been so precarious that Jessica had been afraid to give her daughter the love she carried inside. Instead, she guarded her as if she were a precious jewel to be protected from evil spirits. She knew that she would go to the ends of the earth to protect her daughter and was ever vigilant against any one or any thing that could harm her.

Life at *Inverrigan* had quelled her fears but she was still on guard against any sudden change of circumstance that might once again throw them back into the abyss.

'Mum, your master is calling,' May joked as her mother moved towards the house.

Jessica winced with a moment's pain. She knew her daughter had meant it in jest. Still it hurt. If she let herself, she could be jealous of the girl's advantages, but instead she was happy that May had had such a well provided for, carefree life. It was worth the little humiliations.

She stood beside Douglas, looking over the happy gathering.

'Everything seems to have gone well.'

'Yes. You've done a great job, Jess. I hope the young minx appreciates it. But come inside. I have important matters I want to discuss with you.'

'You sound serious. Is anything wrong?'

'No, no. But it is serious. It concerns our future.'

Jessica's heart skipped a beat at the word "our". Was he, at last, going to legitimise the relationship that had existed between them?

'I've turning forty-one, Jess. I've got to stop playing the happy bachelor and get down to producing an heir.'

'You mean…?'

Douglas was not a cruel man but got some pleasure from the look of expectation he saw in her eyes.

'No, Jess. That horse bolted long ago. Good God woman, I've hardly had sex with you a dozen times in the last five years. You're too old, Jess. I need youth. I need new blood. But don't worry you will be looked after. After all you will be the mother of the bride.'

She stared in horror. 'Douglas, you do not mean . . .'

'Yes I do. You know how much I love her. Why do you think I condone her little indulgences? Yes, Jess. Your beautiful daughter will make a fitting wife for me.'

'But you can't.'

'Oh yes I can. I can do anything I like. She's a woman now, Jess. Nothing illegal about it.'

'But she is so young.' Jessica felt like someone drowning in a pond, but she had to struggle, for May's sake.

'Yes, she is, isn't she?' Douglas watched his chosen one, frolicking with her friends. 'Young and nubile, and what a beautiful Mrs Douglas Henderson she will make.'

'But what about our ... er ... past?'

'That's it girl, past – gone – forgotten. Just because I've slept with the mother don't preclude me from marrying the daughter. No rule against it that I have heard of. Not even in the Bible.'

She could feel the weeds pulling her under. She made one last effort.

'What if she does not want to marry an old man?'

'Not old, Jess, in the prime of life. What every girl needs. Callow young bloods don't know what to do with a woman. It's fumble, fumble, in and out and all for their own satisfaction. A man with experience knows how to please a woman, eh Jess? You certainly thought so.'

Jessica knew she was beaten, but she tried one last time. 'And if she refuses?'

'Refuses? Never. But that is where you come in. You're her mother. You, more than anyone, can help her see the advantages such a marriage will give her.'

'And if I am not willing to help?'

The genial smile was gone. The hard business face that had stared down many an opponent across a boardroom table replaced it. 'Let's stop dancing around the problem. To help clear your mind, let me paint you a scenario – you and May, out on the street, no money, no home. How are you and your precious daughter going to live then, eh? You'd be back knocking on the door, begging to be let in, in less than a week.

And Jessica knew it was true. Neither of them could survive without his patronage.

He gave her a pitying look. 'You lose, Jess. You lose all around. I am going to marry May. You are going to smooth the way and she is going to say yes.'

CHAPTER 7

ADELAIDE

Joel rang me that night. Mum took the call and was quite excited that I was getting a phone call from a boy, but I dashed her hopes by telling her that he was ringing about some maths that I was having trouble with.

'Is he good at maths?'

'Brilliant,' I assured her.

She sighed. 'Your father wasn't any good at maths at all. He was much more interested in the Humanities.'

So now Joel has two strikes against him. He is a Forbes and a mathematician. I'm beginning to like him more and more.

Unfortunately his investigation hadn't got him any further than mine

'I came up with a cunning plan,' he told me, 'I thought I'd pump my father to see if I could get a date we could work from.'

'And?'

'Well the conversation went a bit like this – "Dad, when did our family come to Australia?"

"Let me see. It was after the First World War. About 1920 I think."

"So, there weren't any Forbes here before then?"

"I'm sure there were, but not any related to us. Grandpa did have an Uncle, who sponsored him, but I think that was on his mother's side. I could check, if you like?"

"No. I was just interested in the Forbes. Is the uncle the reason why he went to Queensland?"

"I believe so. But what has brought on this sudden interest in family history?"

"Nothing really. But you know those signs people are holding up – Go back to where you came from – Well that got us started on a discussion at school about where we all came from and how long we'd been here. Joe Foster says his family came out on the Buffalo, so that makes him at least ten or twelve generations, he says."

"I'm sorry son, but you're only fourth on the Forbes side, though you may go back further on your mother's side. Why don't you ask her?"

"Nar. It's not important. Just something to brag about, I guess."

"How times have changed. When I was young, people used to boast about how English, or in my case Scottish, they were, but since the great influx of migrants we are busy establishing how Australian we are. Once the convict stain was a curse, now it's a badge of honour."

'But I had lost interest. I had a date. Unless the feud went back to the old country, the 20's would be the place to start.

'Thanks to Dr Google I began researching grisly murders of the 20s in Brisbane. But the good doctor has let us down. I tried Famous Murders Timeline but couldn't find one. I changed the title to Queensland but no better result. Major Crimes had no murders in the whole of Queensland for the 20's, 30's or 40's.

Either they were the most law-abiding state in the commonwealth or else only common murders happened there. Under Unsolved Crimes the earliest seemed to be 1976. Cold Cases was not much better, but I did notice that females were over represented in these. So it's not going to be so easy. A more tailored investigation is required I guess and that will require precious study time.

'Why don't we try researching newspapers of the time?'

'Yeah, when we get a closer date. I don't fancy going through every newspaper headline from 1920. Perhaps it happened after your grandmother was born? That would narrow it down a bit. But we haven't got much time Sal if you want me to partner you. You know, this is beginning to sound like a trailer for a Disney movie. "Will the handsome prince take Cinderella to the ball or will Wicked Grandmother Flora intervene?"

I was still smiling after I put the phone down. Who wouldn't want to be partnered by a guy like that?

The call got me thinking. Grandmother was sixty-eight last birthday, so that means she must have been born in 1940. That was in the middle of the war. Funny she's always going on about battles that happened hundreds of years ago so I guess "noble Douglas" couldn't have done anything great for his country during that war. I wonder, was he even a soldier? I bet he wasn't or there would have been a portrait of him in uniform on the wall or at least a display of medals he had won.

I'd love to ask but then I might upset Flora. I could ask Mum but as she's a pacifist she has probably never asked herself. However, 1940 might be a good time to start. I wonder what papers were being published in Queensland then? I doubt a simple murder would have made the national headlines, unless if it had been a particularly gruesome one.

I don't know why but thinking about my Great Grandmother's name got me thinking about wedding photos. The only one in the house it that of Grandmother and Grandy Archy, a very stiff affair. Grandmother was only slightly taller than Grandy but she dominates the scene. She is wearing a rather plain satin dress, fitted to the waist then flowing out in a swirling mass and ending in a train, which, in the picture, has been swept to the front to settle at her feet. Only the tips of her white shoes can be seen peeping from it. The neckline has been cut only low enough to show the triple row of pearls, a Henderson heirloom no doubt. The veil is held back by another cluster of pearls. She has a small bouquet of three white lilies with green stems. Those and the yellow stamens of the flowers are the only colour other than white in the whole outfit. If the white was to signify purity then she must have been on a par with one of those vestal virgins in ancient Rome.

Grandy looks very handsome in full morning suit with, you guessed it, white gloves and a white carnation in his buttonhole

So, if the Hendersons were not averse to wedding photos, why isn't there one of Douglas and his bride?

And, now that I come to think of it, why isn't there one of Mum's wedding? The only photo of Mum and Dad together was taken on the Berlin Wall when they went there to help demolish it. In all the rest, and there's not many, I'm there too. At least she's alive so I can ask her.

'Mum, why aren't there any photos of your wedding?'

'That's because there isn't one. Your Dad and I never got

married.'

'What!'

'Don't be so shocked. People have been living together long before you lot thought it cool. We never made an issue of it. We didn't need a piece of paper to prove we were committed. We really did mean to do it when you came along, but we always thought there would be plenty of time.' Her eyes started to glaze. 'We never realised there would be so little.'

I knew I had opened a wound and, respecting her privacy, left her to grieve in peace. This may make me appear hard but I really hardly remember my father.

If I had a father figure it was Grandy and I grieve for him still.

Could it have been a similar grieving that made Great Grandfather destroy every image of his wife?

But still, it is as if she has been airbrushed out of family story. Even if she was only a baby when her mother died, why doesn't Grandmother ever mention her? She speaks fondly about her nurse Jess who seemed to have been like a family retained or something. Surely she would have told Grandmother something about her mother?

CHAPTER 8

BRISBANE

Jessica waited until Douglas was away on his triennial trip west, to inspect what was left of his father's empire. It was now a third of what it had been. It had nearly disappeared during the 'long drought', but they had managed to survive and still owned some of the best land on the Darling Downs.

There were two stations, Appin, run by a manager, and Lochaber, run by his younger brother, Charles. Three times a year Douglas visited them to check the books, sort out problems and give a final decision on future development. He was a good manager and had seen the merit in diverting money into enterprises other than sheep but the depression of the thirties had hit him hard. He had invested much of the family wealth in real estate in Brisbane but, with so many out of work, people could not pay their rents. At first there were foreclosures but, as there were no new tenants to take their place, he found it better to keep the buildings occupied even if no money passed hands. At least it kept out vandals.

The wool market fell and there was no money in sheep. Like everyone else they began selling more sheep but with surplus stock and a depressed market there was little money in that. In the end they kept only the breeding stock, took whatever they could for the rest and tightened their belts until good times returned.

But now things were on the up and up. His act of generosity had paid off. He now he had a group of loyal tenants, real estate was booming, wool prices rising and new meat exports developing, and for the last couple of years the weather had been kind. Douglas could relax again. It gave him special pleasure to think that he had protected his father's legacy. Charles was happy to leave the business side of things to his big brother. He often joked, "I'm a farmer not a financier.' To date Charles had gone along with their father's will –it had always been the Henderson way – because Douglas was a bachelor.

We'll see if the news of my nuptials takes the smile from his face, Douglas thought.

He had said to Jessica, just before he left, 'Just remember Jess, I am going to announce the engagement as soon as I return. Make sure the girl's up to the mark.'

Jessica had put off the dreaded task for as long as she could, but Douglas would be back soon. Today she would have to persuade her daughter to accept Douglas' proposal. Of course there would be wailing and weeping but she would have plenty of time to get used to it before his return.

May's reaction was one of disbelief. 'But Mother, you cannot be serious? Marry Uncle Douglas? Marry an old man, a man I have always looked on as a father? It would be like incest.'

'You have always been fond of him.'

'As a kind uncle, yes, not as a prospective husband. Why are you even suggesting it?'

'Because it has to be, Douglas loves you and he wants you for his wife. Any other woman would be over the moon at such a proposal.'

'Any other old, middle-aged woman. If you think he is such a good catch, why don't you marry him yourself?'

'Because he does not want me. He wants you.'

May was too caught up in her own predicament to hear the sadness in her mother's voice.

'Well, he can't have me.'

'Yes he can, darling. He is Douglas Henderson and he can have whatever he wants.'

'So you say. Then he is going to miss out this time. I will tell him to his face.'

'And he will tell you to go, and take your mother with you. We will be out on the streets with nothing.'

'He wouldn't?'

'Oh yes, he would.'

'But you said he loves me.'

'And he does, in his way. But it has to be his way or nothing. He would see you dead rather than have you defy him.' It was only then that May began to realise the seriousness of the situation. She struggled to find a solution. 'We could go to friends.'

Jessica shook her head sadly. 'What friends do we have who are not first his friends? And even if we could find someone to take us in, how would we survive? We have no money and no way of earning any. When your father died I was alone. If it had not have been for Douglas I would have finished up on the streets. The influenza epidemic had killed both my parents and Darby had driven away any friends I had had before I married. Douglas saved us both from destitution. Gave us a good home, respectability and has showered you with luxuries all your life.'

'Because he wanted to marry me.'

'No. That is not true. At first he helped me because of his friendship with Darby. He tried to be a father to you for his sake. But over the years he has developed a genuine love for you. You must believe that. If you are just kind to him he will give you everything.'

'But marriage Mother? How can I marry an old man?'

'He is not so old. In his prime of life, some would say. Marriage is not like in the fairy books, May. I married a young man and my life was hell. I know the war was to blame for most of it but, looking back, I doubt your father would have been much of a husband anyway. And I can tell you, the romance was gone pretty quickly. At least, with Douglas you know what you are getting and he will be good to you.'

May could see her mother was trying to advise her wisely. 'Must I mother?'

'I am afraid you must, Darling.'

Then the tears came, from both of them. But tears dry up and by the time Douglas returned, May would be ready to accept his proposal. Jessica was already making plans for the wedding.

CHAPTER 9

Unbeknown to her mother, May had made some plans of her own.

She had eventually accepted the logic of her mother's argument, but she was young enough to have dreams, dreams of romance, of courtship and of the Wedding Night. She still wanted the handsome, young man to sweep her off her feet, to fulfil all the romantic steps of courtship that she and her friends whispered about. She wanted to fill her wedding night with passion.

How could she expect that with old Uncle Douglas? But she wanted it and she was going to have it. She had about fourteen days to make it all come true. She laid her plan of campaign with as much care as any general.

When *Inverrigan* was built a small, octagonal building, known as the summerhouse, was built in a secluded section of the garden. It had a wide shady roof and the eight wooden louvers caught any passing breeze. It had been a retreat where Ebilin could sit and read on stifling days when she was well enough, and where May and her friends played "house" when they were young. This would be the place where May would carry out her plan.

First she contrived an accidental meeting with Willie. She

tried every coquettish gesture she had ever learned and was thrilled to see the effect they had on the young man. By the time they parted she could feel the power she had over him.

Fortuitously, that Saturday they were to meet socially at an evening entertainment at the home of one of their friends. By design they found themselves alone, under a tree, away from prying eyes.

William could not believe his luck. May let him kiss her, gently at first, then more urgently. His hands strayed to her pert, little breasts and he marvelled at his power as he felt her nipples rising at his touch.

'No, Willie, no.' She pushed him away, reluctantly, but the spell was broken. His own body had responded and he felt a stab of pain at her rejection. By the time he had recovered himself she was walking back towards the others.

What had he done? Why had he behaved so recklessly? Would she ever speak to him again?

May had recovered her composure and was as friendly with him as she was with all their circle of friends. She had forgiven him, he hoped.

Five days later he received a dinner invitation from Jessica. May was having a mid-week tea for six friends. Could he find himself free to even the numbers?

Could he? He would walk over hot coals to be there. Had May planned the uneven numbers especially so that he would be invited?

William did his best to join in the general banter, but he could not take his eyes off her. Was it his imagination or did they manage to brush against each other by design? And were there any secret message in her eyes as she made such a display of discussing the recent refurbishing of the summerhouse?

He got his answer just before he was leaving. 'Willie,' she whispered, 'I must see you alone. Leave with the others, but come back later. I will be waiting in the summerhouse.'

He could hardly breathe. He found an excuse to refuse Gerard and David's suggestion that they make a night of it, then agonized over what 'later' could mean. Just before ten he hurried though the gates of *Inverrigan* and slipped into the darkness of the summerhouse. Was he too early, too late?

'Willie, Willie,' May materialised out of the shadows and threw herself into his arms. They began to kiss passionately

William had never got beyond a few stolen kisses with any girl before, but nature seemed to have prepared him. Soon they were entwined on the new cane lounge and he was exploring her partly undressed body.

Though May had never been in this situation before she seemed to know by instinct what would please her most. When she felt William's hesitation her hands gently guided him.

They were both inexperienced and the encounter was short. In fact May, as the body underneath, felt quite uncomfortable. Still, it had been accomplished. She didn't really know what all the fuss was about. She had enjoyed the preliminaries much more than the deed. But, at least, now she was a woman.

Willie had poured all he had into the encounter and lay, exhausted on top of her for a time. Then the enormity of what he had done roused him.

'May, oh my Darling May.' Tears of joy trickled down his face. 'Oh, May, did you enjoy it? Did I go too far? Did I go further than you wanted?'

'No, silly boy, it was lovely. But would you mind moving so

that I can sit up. It's quite uncomfortable here. '

As she rearranged her clothes she noticed drops of blood on one of the cushions.

'Look Willie, you have taken my maidenhead.' She had been told all about this by her friends, but poor William was totally ignorant.

'Oh, God May. What have I done? Have I hurt you? We must get married at once.'

'Silly Willie. I'm not hurting at all. But you know what this means. I will be yours forever. Now come and sit beside me. I have something very important to say.' She patted the seat. 'I want you to listen carefully. Don't interrupt because what I am going to tell you is very important to us both.'

William was her slave. He would have done anything for her. Sitting beside her was such a small request. She had his full attention.

'You may not know, but when my father died, mother and I were penniless. Uncle Douglas took us into his house out of the goodness of his heart, even though we were not related to him. He is only my uncle in name. Without him I don't know whether I would be alive today.'

She paused to let these facts sink in then went on before he could interrupt. 'He wants me to be his wife'

She raised her finger to his lips to stop the protest coming from his mouth. 'No, don't say anything. Just listen. It is his wish and I am going to abide by it. I am doing this in gratitude to him and for my mother's future.'

May felt very virtuous at this moment. She wished she could see herself, so noble, so self-sacrificing. The image almost brought tears to her eyes.

William was devastated. "You cannot, May. You cannot sacrifice your life like this.'

'Yes, I can Willie. I can and I will. But I want you to remain my one, true friend. Others may make their own judgement but I want you to promise me that you will always love me, as I will you. For Willie, you are my first love and I will always have you in my heart.'

'I will not let you do this.'

'Then you do not truly love me.' May pushed his protective arm away. 'You would destroy me rather than let another have my body.'

'May, my darling May, it is not your body that I want. It is you, your beautiful spirit, your gentle ways.'

'But you already have these, Willie. You have my heart. Think, Willie, if I do not marry Uncle Douglas he will throw me out and my mother too. And, though you are too noble to have such thoughts, he will also destroy you. He will make sure you never succeed at anything you do. Can't you see that I am doing this for you too.'

Willie looked in adoration at this beautiful girl, willing to sacrifice herself for others. May could see she had won the argument. He would make no trouble and she had won his undying devotion. Who knew what the future held? She might need it some day.

A hundred arguments came to his mind but the determined look in May's beautiful, blue eyes silenced him. She was deadly serious. Nothing he could say or do would change her mind. She was not only the most beautiful girl in the world she was also the most noble. Eventually he surrendered.

'May, I know my heart is broken. You are the bravest, most heroic girl in the whole world. I am not worthy of you. But if you are willing to make such a sacrifice I will too. I swear, by all I hold dear, that I will never marry anyone but you.'

'Thank you, Willie.'

What else could a girl say to such a noble declaration?

CHAPTER 10

Jessica answered Douglas' raised eyebrow with a nod. Soon she left him alone with her daughter.

May knew, and Douglas knew she knew, still formalities had to be observed. The young girl stood in a shaft of sunlight from the window, eyes downcast, hands clasped lightly behind her back. She had practised this stance in front of her bedroom mirror, submissive but not servile.

As he took in the scene so carefully prepared for him, Douglas felt an odd sensation. His heart began to race and he had difficulty breathing. She is so young, he thought. He experienced a new emotion, one he had not felt since he was a young man. This was not lust. This was genuine love. It took him completely by surprise. His desire was not to possess her, though he planned to do that too, but to love and cherish, just as it said in the marriage vows. This was real love, the stuff of legends. Made mere men demigods. The very best of literature and art was inspired by feelings such as this.

For the first time in his life, he felt unsure, afraid almost. He thought of a phrase, from Shakespeare, perhaps; *I am undone.* That was how he felt, "undone". He had thought of himself as her master, now he felt more like a slave. If I take this step, he asked himself, if I actually ask the question, will I still be my own man?

Was this why I have remained single for so long?

The long pause was too much for May. She raised her head.

'Do you want to ask me something, Uncle?'

The spell was broken.

The minx, he thought. Well, here goes.

'Yes darling girl. Yes I do, and you know what it is. Well, what is your answer?'

A half smile played around her lips. 'How can I answer a question if it isn't asked?'

She had prepared a pretty answer. A simple "yes" would have been a terrible letdown.

'Are you playing with me, May?' He had seen through her guile. 'But all right, I suppose you deserve a proper proposal ... ahem ... Dear May, I have long loved you, first as a daughter but now as a beautiful woman whom I wish to make my wife. May Swann, will you do me the honour of becoming my wife?'

'Thank you, my dearest Uncle for the great honour you have bestowed on me. I love you too and will be happy to become Mrs Douglas Henderson.'

Douglas breathed a sigh of relief. He had not realised it, but some small part of him had been afraid that at the last minute she would say no.

He held out his arms. 'Well, Mrs Henderson to be, come and kiss your intended and, in that position, I give my first order. From this time on you may call me any endearing term you wish but I never want to hear again the one starting with U.'

'I will try.'

May sank into his shoulder, which was certainly manly. He bent to kiss her, gently at first, then with passion. May found she enjoyed it, and would have liked to respond but remembering she was the inexperienced maiden, pushed him gently away.

'Oh . . .er . . Douglas, please.'

'May. My beautiful May.' He held her at arm's length, enraptured by her beauty. 'I'm sorry. In my eagerness I forgot you are still a girl. I will do my best to control myself but I hope the engagement is not a long one. After all, I am only mortal. Now go and call your mother, whom I am sure is hovering close by. We have a wedding to plan and the sooner the better.'

The engagement announcement, when it appeared in the social pages of the Brisbane Courier Mail, caused a minor sensation. Opinions were mixed between whether Douglas was a "lucky bugger" or a "randy old man", whether May was a "lucky young girl" or a "scheming puss" but the general consensus was that Jessica a was a "gold digger, sacrificing her daughter for her own ends."

However, during the social events that followed the announcement, the couple were so caring of each other that everyone agreed that "it was a match made in heaven."

May blossomed amid all the attention. With a little behind the scenes advice from her mother she proved herself sophisticated beyond her years. In the charming hostess she was becoming, her friends saw little of the giddy girl they had known. Douglas was delighted to have so many bright, young people running in and out of his establishment.

'Another advantage of a young bride,' he confided to Jessica, 'so many young people with their fresh ideas. I don't know why we excluded them for so long. They make me feel young again. I feel much more confident about the future when I listen to them. Of course they have a lot to learn, but they will have some things to teach us in a few years. You wouldn't believe it but one young man was telling me about a new American invention called Television. It's like the movies, but it's in real time and he claims that it won't be long before there is one in every home. Can't see it myself but then that's what they said about indoor plumbing.'

Douglas was very proud of the new plumbing arrangements at *Inverrigan,* so much nicer to turn on a tap and set your own temperature rather than to have a servant fill the tub up with scalding water and wait for it to cool. And it was a blessing not to have to use the thunder bucket under the bed.

Douglas's friends were surprised at how tolerant he had become. 'I do believe,' one old adversary commented, 'the old boy's got a heart after all.' To which his companion replied, 'It will only last until he beds her.'

The engagement was short, only three months, just long enough to arrange what was to be the wedding of the year. Though Jessica, as the mother of the bride, penned most of the invitations, Douglas took especial pleasure in writing a personal letter to Charles.

Dear Brother Charles,

No doubt the news of my intended nuptials has reached even your remote corner of the state. It would give May and me great pleasure if yourself, Molly and the two boys could attend our wedding. I wish to make a further request, that you attend me as best man.

As you don't get many chances to visit the big smoke, let me extend the invitation further. As May and I will be leaving for an extended honeymoon in New Zealand, feel free to sojourn at Inverrigan for as long as you please.

He would liked to have added - enjoy it while you can, because when I produce my sons, you will never own it.

Jessica and May had decided on three bridesmaids, but grooms caused a headache, Douglas was all for asking his old friends until Jessica managed to persuade him that to have three pretty girls on the arm of three old cronies wouldn't look good in the wedding photos. Charles was fine. It was a given, but two more?

He compromised by asking the son of his friend and neighbour, George Reid, and May, to satisfy a whim, insisted on William Forbes.

CHAPTER 11

The family name, Reid, resounds through the pages of English law. They had a fine knowledge of, and regard for, the role of jurisprudence in the developing legal system that had made England. And not only in England. Wherever the empire went it took its system of law, to supplant earlier, tribal lore or inferior legal systems. Where the law went, Reids went too.

A member of the family had been appointed to the colony of New South Wales in the early 1800s and, when Queensland became a separate colony in 1859, William Reid was appointed as a senior judge. His son Albert had followed in his father's footsteps and it was he who had built Westmere, a lovely home in the Queen Anne style, on a property adjoining *Inverrigan.* He and Douglas had become great friends. Douglas appreciated Albert's legal intelligence and often consulted him on matters of law. He was a man who listened often but expressed his own opinion rarely. He could see through all the chatter and did not bare fools gladly. A man after my own heart, Douglas thought.

Albert had a son and it was assumed, by all, that the name Reid would live on in the annals of Australian law.

But as any breeder of horses will tell you, centuries of breeding does not always produce a winner, and Gerard would prove to be the offspring that brought the family down.

He was handsome, tall, athletic, with fine features and a wayward head of hair that, in spite of his mother's constant grooming, fell across his forehead. But, instead of appearing dishevelled, it gave him an air of roguish charm that captivated everyone who met him. It was only those who had a closer acquaintance, such as his teachers, who recognised the shallow nature that lay behind the charming face.

Of course his mother would hear none of this but Albert, when he began to pay attention to his son, began to become suspicious of the cunning that had steered his son through several potential disasters. As the boy was nearing the end of his schooling Albert contemplated, not the law, but the army as a career for him. It would teach him discipline, order and a respect for the law. Both Gerard and his mother were totally opposed to the idea.

Had Albert known about his son's extracurricular activities he would have been much more worried and come up with a more drastic solution than a commission in a peacetime army.

When Gerard was still in primary school he had learnt that people had secrets and, if you became privy to them, they would be willing to give you things on the promise that you would not tell. At the beginning it was only little things, like half a pie or a special football card but by the time he became a boarder at Brisbane Grammar, on a strict allowance, this skill helped to supplement his income. And his victims were not only his fellow students. In year eleven he discovered a teacher in a compromising position. He had struck gold. A regular amount began to appear in his bank account. Not a lot. He never asked for a large amount, just that it was regular.

He now knew the indiscretions that were best to look out for, infidelity, illicit drug use and the daddy of them all, homosexuality. As soon as he had an inclination of a possible victim he would pursue them, search their mail, even lay traps for them. Sometimes it was a waste of effort but his success rate would have been quite an achievement for a trained detective.

By the time he was in university he needed those constant deposits, for he had developed a habit of his own; gambling. Though he had some successes he was not as clever at picking winners as he was in finding losers. He needed those constant sums to settle his gambling debts. He mainly bet on horses, but cards played a part. Once or twice he had been a little late in settling his account and felt fear. He knew what happened to anyone who welshed on a deal.

He had known May all his life and for some time had seen her as a possible wife and provider of future income. Of course he knew of William's passion for May and was amused to see her respond. She was a notorious flirt. But he never, for one moment thought of William as a rival. After all William was a nobody, relying on the good will of his uncle to fund his career. He was said to be clever, but when did brains win out over money.

Gerard was quite disappointed when the engagement to Douglas was announced but was pleased to be chosen as a groomsman. He intended to continue their childhood friendship, hoping that, in the future, some advantage might come his way. Surely such a beautiful young girl would not be satisfied with a silly old man, old enough to be her father. Sooner or later, she would slip up and when she did he would be there to profit from it.

CHAPTER 12

ADELAIDE

What's wrong with me? The government has just chosen Quentin Bryce to be our first female Governor General. The highest office in the land, and it's been given to a woman!!! It is a time for all females to show that we are, at least equal, if not superior to any man. The founding mothers of Alexandra Ladies Academy must be cheering from their graves. It's a time for each of us to strive to be the very best woman we can possible be.

And what am I doing? Mooning over a boy like some feather headed thirteen-year-old.

So, I've met a guy that I like, and to date I think he likes me. At least he has agreed to partner me so he must think I'm at least presentable. What's the big deal? It happens to everyone sooner or later.

But why did is this happening to me now? All my girlfriends have had at least one boyfriend. Ellie and Joe have been going together since kindergarten. Most of the others started dating seriously by the time they were fifteen. But me? All my "dreamboats" are plastered on my wall. My mother had drummed it into me from an early age that life starts when you go away to university, and the way to get there is to get excellent marks in matric. That way you gain fabulous scholarships and can choose a uni. as far away from Adelaide as possible. After that the world is your oyster.

'It worked for me' she said. 'It will work for you too.'

So why mess up a good plan now by falling in love and falling behind in my studies?

The fact that I am naturally bright and that lots of girls manage study and a boyfriend was never pointed out to me, so until now, even though I have had the odd crush or two, I have never let it interfere with my busy schedule of music, sport and study. Truth to tell, I'm a bit of a snob when it comes to boyfriends. Only girls with no brains spent their time dreaming about boys. I didn't believe in romantic love. I saw myself a modern day Elizabeth Bennet, in full control of my own life. Now I'm behaving more like silly Lydia.

How could it happen that just when the finishing line is almost in sight I have been smitten? I sit, looking at an open textbook, and all I see is **his** face. I start an essay and find myself making lists of all the things I like about him. Thank goodness I haven't any artistic talent or I'd be drawing aspects of him all over my notebooks. As it is, I can't open a magazine or newspaper with pictures of handsome men without finding similarities with his eyes, his smile, his hair and don't start on bodies. If I could make a list of all the most gorgeous males in the world and roll them into one they would only be a shadow of my beautiful Joel.

But what is this doing to my head? I daydream in lessons. I can't concentrate. I can't sleep at night and we haven't even pashed yet. Is this real or is it all in my head. And what makes me think he feels the same? I've only spoken to him a few times. We haven't even had a date. I was the one who contacted him and that was only to discuss the family secret. Will I even see him after the Formal?

And, if this does become a serious affair and I manage to pull off the miracle and get accepted in Melbourne or Sydney or Perth even, will he want to come with me? Or will I be like my mother, following her love around the world, happy to do his bidding? But I can't bear the thought of being separated from him.

And then there's the family affair. If this mystery is really real, how will it affect me? Will I have to cut all ties with the formidable Flora, say goodbye to Glencoe and do it all on my own? How can two old fogies who died years ago cause strife for two young people in 2008? At least Romeo and Juliette knew why their families hated each other.

I have had no experience with this. Am I just blowing it up into some great romance when it is only a silly, teenage crush?

I have always been the cool one, giving sound advice to my smitten friends and lend them my shoulder to cry on when it all goes belly up. But now that I need a bit of advice myself I'm too proud to confide in them or ask for help. What does that say about me?

I've got to stop this and get down to work. I've got an assignment due on Friday and I've hardly started yet.

I wonder if my great grandmother ever had problems like this?

CHAPTER 13

BRISBANE - 1939

Though the immediate problem of Sudetenland had been settled, Europe was far from a peaceful place. The League of Nations was falling apart. Douglas seemed more and more distracted and new names like Mussolini, Molotov and Churchill were heard often on the six pm news.

More and more he and his friends ruined dinners by talking politics and spent hours in his study arguing the pros and cons of alliances between Germany, Italy and the Soviet Union and Britain, France and Poland. Some of them predicted another war but Douglas still had faith that wisdom would prevail.

'No one is ever going to start an all out war again after the last debacle,' he assured his friends.

'What about Spain?' one argued.

'Well, what can you expect from a country like that? Anyway they've settled that now, and a good thing too. You can't have Communists running the country. Look at Russia.'

Much more pressing to Douglas and his friends was the weather. The summer of '39 had been the hottest on record and in the southern states, especially Victoria, bush fires were raging. The final death toll of 71 appalled the whole nation. It was christened Black Friday.

'God help us if a war began here in summer.' Douglas stated. 'This country is like one huge tinder box,' Douglas stated. 'If it gets much hotter and drier you could start a fire in Cape York and it would burn all the way down to Port Phillip Bay.'

It was all boring, old man talk to May. It was "over there" and had nothing to do with her and the life she was living. She cared nothing for the state of the world at large. She had her own problems.

Month followed month and still she was not pregnant. She could feel her power slipping. Though Douglas never spoke of it openly, she knew he was disappointed. He had ceased trying to instruct her or asking her opinions. He spent more time with his friends, discussing business, or at his club.

He was even more interested in the house extensions than he was in her. In desperation she took her problems to her mother.

'Mother, what is wrong with me? I've tried everything. I've even tried eating pineapple cores and honey in my wine that I read would help, but still no baby. What's to become of me if I don't produce an heir?'

Jessica had been thinking about this problem for some time. She knew the reason.

'I doubt the problem is yours May. I have suspected it for years. Douglas had not been what you would call a celibate man before he married you yet there have been no offspring. I warrant he was not always as careful as he should have been. I believe he cannot produce children. I see no reason at all that it is your fault.'

'Then, what can I do? He'll begin to hate me soon.'

Jessica indicated to her daughter to sit, then sat beside her and patted her hair.

'May, women have been faced with this problem since the dawn of time. Whenever there were no babies the woman was to blame. To suggest to a man that he was incapable of producing offspring is to castrate him, destroy his masculinity, so it was always the woman's fault.'

'So there is nothing I can do?'

'Yes there is and, once again, women have been doing it forever. You must find a fertile male, have him impregnate you, then convince your husband that he is the father.'

'Mother!' May was shocked.

'I know. It is the last advice you expected from me, but it is the only way. But you must be very discreet. In olden days the lady of the manor could rely on the discretion of a servant, but, in your case you must choose wisely and it must be someone you can trust, absolutely.'

That evening, after she had got over the horror of her mother's suggestion in her mind, May came up with a happy solution, one that had been provided by Douglas himself.

'Thank you Douglas,' she whispered into her pillow.

CHAPTER 14

She planned carefully. She must rekindle the torch she knew William still held for her, but it must appear to be of his doing. She would have three weeks in August to carry out her seduction and she had two great reasons why it could not continue – her vulnerability as Douglas' wife and his power to destroy William's future.

She must also convince Douglas that the child was his. There must be no doubt. To accomplish this she began another little subterfuge before he went away.

Douglas,' she began, at breakfast, a few days later, using the "little girl" voice that seemed to arouse him, 'I have a confession to make.'

'What is it May? Overspent your allowance again?' He continued eating.

'No, Douglas, something much more serious' He raised his eyes.

'And please, Darling, before you get all cross, I want you to know I did it for us.'

She had his full attention now. 'Go on.'

'I know I've been a disappointment to you. I know you so want a son and I haven't been able to provide one.'

'May, this is hardly breakfast talk. Can't you save it till the evening.' He was secretly worried that what he had long suspected was true, that he might be infertile.

'No, Douglas. Please hear me out. I have felt, for some time that I might be … er … deficient in some way.' She paused and looked at him with pleading eyes. 'Don't be cross. I consulted a Chinese herbalist.'

'A what?'

'A Chinese herbalist.'

'You let a Chinaman examine you!'

'Only my hands and my eyes. He just looked at my palms and into my eyes.'

Douglas was furious. 'And what did he find?'

'That I am anaemic, that I am too tense and that I do not eat the foods that help procreation.'

'Oh, and what are they?'

'Organ meats, liver and kidney and things like that.' She shuddered. 'You know how I hate them, but I will try to in the future.'

The conversation was beginning to amuse him. 'Good, anything else?'

'Yes, beans, seeds, herbs and worst of all seaweed.'

He burst out laughing. 'Seaweed! And do you intend to go down to the bay each day to graze or will it be parsley and thyme one day and kelp the next.'

'Douglas, please take this seriously. I don't actually have to eat these things. The herbalist has given me some herbs containing all these things. I had to buy a brand new teapot, and each morning I must pour boiling water over them, wait for the water to cool, then drink the whole pot full.'

'And does this concoction taste delicious?'

'If it tastes anything like the smell of the herbs, I don't think so. I won't bring it to the breakfast table.' She could see Douglas was not taking her seriously and was losing interest.

"There was one more thing, Darling, that might please you, oysters. You know how I hate them, won't even try them, Well, he says I should have half a dozen at least twice a week.'

The mention of oysters pricked his interest. It was common knowledge that stout and oysters made a potent brew. Many a man blamed them for an unplanned pregnancy. Perhaps the Orientals knew a thing or two after all. There were certainly enough of them.

'My darling, little wife,' he began lightly, hoping that she would know that he didn't believe in all this nonsense. 'I forgive you for speaking about our problem to strangers. I know you did it for the best of reasons so, if you are willing to drink this dreadful concoction, I will do my part. I will order lambs fry and bacon, devilled kidneys or faggots with gravy every morning for breakfast and we will have stout and oysters at least three times a week.'

May pulled a face then put on a brave smile to show him what she was willing to do to grant his desire.

Edna, the cook was annoyed at this sudden change in the breakfast menu, May made sure that the aroma from the herb mixture was smelt throughout the house, though the contents of the teapot were poured down the toilet, and Douglas approached the project of producing an heir with renewed vigour.

Satisfied that Douglas believed her story May had only one more task to perform. To once again lure William to the summerhouse.

CHAPTER 15

Poor deluded William, he was putty in her hands. A few sighs, the odd tear before her husband left, to suggest that all was not as it seemed in her marriage – a cry on his shoulder, and a secret meeting in the summerhouse after Douglas had left.

May was not stupid enough to believe that one encounter would bring about the desired result. With Jessica's help they met, almost nightly. May had had the foresight to get rid of the cane lounge and replaced it with a soft couch. She found the whole experience delightful.

Though lacking Douglas' experience, William was learning and she enjoyed the role she played as the penitent wife. She never said it in words, but William always felt he was the villain, seducing her away from her chosen destiny. Each day he vowed he would end the affair, but the sight of May, languishing in a chair or strolling listlessly around the garden, and he lost his reserve.

After a fortnight of encounters May believed she had given him every chance, after all, how long does it take a healthy sperm to do its duty. Now she had to begin the delicate manoeuvre of separation.

That evening it began.

'Willie, you know I love you. I will always love you. But this has got to stop. This must be the last time we meet here. I made a solemn vow, before everyone, that I would be faithful to my husband.' May had a mental image of herself, dressed in virginal white, taking her vow. It made her feel quite noble. 'I must honour that vow. Douglas is a good man and I cannot disgrace him.'

'But you don't love him, May.'

'Yes, I do. Not in the way I do you, but I cannot hurt him. Do not try and make me. Do not turn me into a cruel, unfaithful wife. Please, please Willie.'

'You could never be that.'

'Yes. I could be, Willie. I already am. You have persuaded me to betray a man who has always had my welfare at heart. How could I? How could you? I know you are not totally to blame but I am only a weak woman and you should have protected me from myself. How could you?'

Her sobs were quite genuine, but when Willie began to console her, she pushed his arm away. 'No. It must stop now. You once made a vow to me too. Have you forgotten? Be strong for me Willie, please.'

William was torn between love and guilt. He was disgusted with himself. He had taken the opportunity that Douglas had given to show his talents and then betrayed the man by seducing his wife. What kind of a monster was he? And look what he had done to his beloved May.

'Oh, God May, you must hate me. I have taken your innocent affection and used you for my own gratification. I will leave immediately and start again in another state.'

This was not exactly what she had had in mind.

'No, Willie, no. Never say that. How could I live without

knowing you were there, my one, true friend. And you can't leave your work half done. I love the way the black roof, with its frilly iron lace edging flows out from the building. It reminds me of the petticoat of a Spanish gypsy. And the French windows. Oh Willie, you must finish it, make *Inverrigan* the most beautiful residence in Queensland. Do it as a tribute to our love. Every day, when I walk on your veranda, I will think of you and whenever you walk by, you will think of me. Everyone else will think you did it for Douglas but I will know you did it for me.'

May knew she had won the day. Love for her, and pride in his work would stop him from doing anything silly and she still had his undying devotion.

Who knew, she might need it again some day.

May was sure she was pregnant even before she had missed her menses. She felt motherly. Now she had one more job – to announce to Douglas that he was to become a father.

Douglas had not expected to miss May so much. The two weeks, trying to make a baby, had rekindled the romance of early marriage and he was more than willing to continue the experiment.

May created an attractive pose, leaning on the railing of the completed front veranda. As soon as she was sure he had taken in the artistic arrangement, she ran down the steps and flung herself into his arms.

'Douglas, Douglas. I am so glad you are back. I have missed you so much. What do you think of the beautiful front windows?' She prattled on, as she had done when a child, anxious to see the present he would always bring.

He was surprised at the degree of desire he felt. He could

have taken her then and there but restrained himself until after the welcome home meal Jessica had prepared.

'That was excellent, Jess. Better than most I've eaten on the road. But it has been a long journey so, with my wife's permission,' he squeezed May's hand, 'I would like to retire early.'

'Of course, Douglas. I understand.' He did not notice the knowing look she gave her daughter.

May's eagerness took his breath away. He could hardly restrain himself as he went through his nightly ablution. The vision of May, in white satin, her fair hair floating over her shoulders, eager eyes shining and arms open wide to receive his embrace, transported him to another level. Their coupling was in turn, torrid and tender. Douglas was amazed at his own stamina, and May was impressed.

But eventually weariness took over. He lay back and closed his eyes but just before he slipped into sleep, May leant over and whispered, 'Douglas, I have a secret to tell you. I am not yet certain, but I think the herbs worked.'

He sat up, all desire for sleep gone, but she had turned over and was already in the arms of Morpheus. He spent the rest of the night switching between elation and worry. What did she mean, wasn't sure, was it possible that, at last there would be a son to inherit, could the torrid love making have done any damage, if she was?

On the 3rd of September all over the country Australians stopped to hear a message from Prime Minister Menzies that "in consequence of persistence by Germany in her invasion of Poland, Great Britain had declared war upon her and that, as a result, Australia also is at war."

Douglas' prediction that the great powers would come to their senses had been wrong but it did not dampen the elation he felt when May confirmed the good news. The miracle had happened. The Chinese medicine had worked and there would soon be another Henderson to continue the line.

For Jessica, the news that Australia was at war again brought back nightmares that she thought were banished from her mind. Surely the monster called Empire was not going to devour another generation of young men. She thanked God that May was married and Douglas would be too old to serve. This war would have no effect on their lives, but she grieved for all the young lives that would be sacrificed and for the young women who would be made widows or be destined to become old maids.

For May the goings on overseas hardly registered against the happiness she felt now that she was to become the mother of the next Henderson. Her future was secure.

CHAPTER 16

1940

May had an easy pregnancy. There was minimum morning sickness and her pretty ankles did not swell. However, as the little bump grew, she mourned her slender figure. Maternity clothes were dull and frumpy and her back hurt. Though she would never have shown herself in public looking as she did, she resented the social expectation that she retire for several months.

By the fifth month she was bored, irritable and listless. Douglas, who was unused to playing second fiddle, found his life being constantly directed by an irrational, young woman, and at a time when world events dictated that he spend time dissecting the news with his friends.

If he was too often at the Club it was, 'Douglas Henderson, now that you have made me pregnant, you abandon me. All day I wait for you to come and tell me that you still love me.'

When he stayed at home it was 'Douglas, the smell of your cigar is making me sick.'

'I only smoke on the veranda.'

'But the smell of it is in your breath and on your clothing.'

'Would you have me give it up?'

'No. That would only make you hate me more. I know you already hate the big, fat lump I have become.' And then the tears would start, not the gentle, dewy drops that had charmed him but torrents that blotched her cheeks and reddened her eyes.

He went to Jessica for advice. 'Jess, I don't know how much more of this I can take. Do all women carry on like this?'

'I know, Douglas, she is a bit overwrought. But remember, she is little more than a child herself. Young people these days put so much value on their appearance. She thinks, because she is no longer attractive, you will no longer love her.'

'That is ridiculous. She is carrying my child. Every time I look at her rounded stomach all I can think of is, "that is my son in there". But she is driving me to distraction. Perhaps I should go away until after the child is born.'

'No, Douglas. You have wanted this for so long. You must be here when the baby comes. Don't worry. I will speak to her. Perhaps a small gift, a piece of jewellery, might reassure her that you still care.'

Jessica spoke to her daughter. 'May, you have got to stop these tantrums. You are not the first woman in the world to carry a child. The discomfort you feel now will all be forgotten when you hold your baby in your arms.'

'But I'm so sick of sitting here, looking at this lump.'

'Of course you are. But there is no reason for you to sit around. In fact it is not good for you. You need exercise, my girl, exercise for your body and for your mind. You must take up a hobby that will get you out and about.'

'But, Mother, pregnant women are not allowed to be seen in public.'

'Rubbish. Maybe not at the social garden parties you used to like so much, but walking in the park, visiting married friends, why you might even take driving lessons. Lots of young women even have their own cars these days.'

'But what if I have an accident?'

'Stop 'butting' and pull yourself together or, son or not, you will lose your husband and then where will you be?'

May took her mother's words to heart and found a new energy. Douglas forbade the idea of driving, but she threw herself enthusiastically into planning a new garden, and took over the furnishing of the new verandas, with the same enthusiasm she had had when designing her clothes. She treated each area as separate rooms, reception at the front, sitting room on the river side and her personal retreat on the other.

Not only did she have representatives from various establishments visit her with samples but made several trips into the city to inspect showrooms. She was told she had excellent taste. She thought she might become more interested in interior decoration after the baby was born. She knew Douglas would never allow her to actually go into business but perhaps she could become a silent partner. She would discuss the idea with William.

The midwife had been installed at the beginning of the ninth month, just in case May had an early birth but the family doctor was expected to be there for the actual delivery, or to be contacted if there were complications. Dr Rivers, knowing Douglas' medical history better than Douglas did himself, kept his council, but was secretly very interested in seeing the 'miracle' baby, made possible by Chinese herbs.
Though he had been longing for this day, Douglas was dreading

the actual process itself. His friends teased him with stories of screaming and wailing, of waiting outside the room while women ran back and forth with hot water. There was also the fear of something going wrong. Though modern medicine had more than halved the mortality rate there were still deaths of both mothers and babies. No wonder most men did their best to be absent, or to retire with a bottle of scotch until the ordeal was over.

But he believed himself made of sterner stuff and was determined to be awake and sober to greet the next heir to the Henderson clan.

May's labour began on the 20th of June. Though it was long, May endured it with fortitude until the last half hour. Then it became unendurable. She screamed. She cried. She even used words that Jessica hadn't suspected she knew, but eventually the longed for child arrived. May, lying exhausted, heard a tiny cry. She felt a great surge of joy and held out her arms.

'Please, please, give me my baby. Let me hold him in my arms.'

Jessica took the precious bundle and handed it to her. 'Darling, you have a beautiful baby daughter.'

May was just about to take the baby when Jessica's words penetrated.

'A daughter! No, no.' She pushed the little bundle away. 'No, Mother. It has to be a boy. Douglas will be furious.' She burst into uncontrollable sobs.

'What is wrong with you?' Dr Rivers demanded. But May was incapable of speech.

'It's Douglas,' Jessica explained. 'He has been so sure that it would be a boy. I don't know how he will take the disappointment.' Jessica was now holding her precious grandchild close, afraid for its future.

Rivers was furious and stormed into the nearby room where Douglas, having heard the baby's cry, was waiting to be summoned into the birth room.

'Douglas,' Rivers thundered, 'your young wife, who has just given birth to your child is crying her heart out. This should be the happiest moment of her life but she is devastated because she fears your reaction to the news that you have a daughter.'

'A daughter?' Douglas felt he had received a heavy blow.

'Yes, a daughter, a beautiful, healthy girl. What kind of man are you to reject such a gift and terrify your wife?'

Douglas collapsed back onto the chair he had been sitting on. 'A daughter? I never gave that a thought. A daughter!' As the news penetrated his brain he pulled himself together. 'But I'm not angry, only surprised – but a daughter – a daughter will be grand. She will be like a little mother for the ones to follow. Poor May. I must reassure her at once.'

Dr Rivers stood aside as Douglas strode into the room. 'May, May,' he said as he hurried to her bedside. 'Stop this crying, my dear. You should be laughing. Why did you think I would not welcome a daughter?'

He sat on the edge of the bed to console her. May nestled into his chest and the sobbing subsided. 'You really don't mind, Douglas?'

'Silly girl, of course I don't. Now will someone introduce me to my daughter.'

Jessica had pacified the crying child who now slept peacefully in her arms. She handed the bundle to Douglas.

He peered at the tiny face, half hidden by the rug. He pushed it aside, the better to see, and in so doing touched the soft, warm cheek. Something akin to an electric shock travelled up his arm and settled in his heart. And then, as if to cement her power over him, the baby opened her eyes and gave him a steady look.

When he recounted this incident he was always told that a newborn's eyes cannot focus, but he knew better. She had looked him in the eye. An understanding passed between them. She was his and he was hers and the bond would never be broken.

May broke the spell. 'Douglas, what are we going to call her? We never thought of a girl's name'

Douglas looked at his daughter. He knew immediately what she would be called.

'Flora, Flora Jean, Jean after my mother and Flora for the brave girl who saved the Bonny Prince. '

Jessica's own introduction to motherhood had been overshadowed by fear and anxiety. She had been afraid to embrace the happiness she felt for fear that that, too, would be taken from her. It was not until Douglas had befriended her and her daughter that she began to believe that they had a future.

But there was no cloud over this birth. She could love this child unconditionally, knowing that its future was safe. Her one desire was to care for Flora, to hold her, bath and change her, watch her sleeping moments and relieve any pain caused by wind or rash. She was the first to respond to the faintest cry, the slightest sign of discomfort.

CHAPTER 17

Douglas, a busy man, could not spend as much time with his daughter as he wished, but managed to squeeze in a little time with her each day. And every day he saw a change in complexion, a thickening of the downy fuzz that covered her head or the endless activities of her hands and feet. He sat, fascinated, as Flora's eyes followed his finger as he moved it in and out of her vision. It was he who first heard the happy sound she made that he knew was laughter and the first to notice that the growing thatch had a tinge of red.

'She's going to have red hair, May, just like my mother. Red hair and blue eyes. She's a Highlander for sure.'

May enjoyed the new status motherhood had given her - the visits, the presents, the cards of congratulations. Everybody of importance in Brisbane and beyond had sent messages of good will. There were congratulations and the present of a beautiful, lace, christening gown from Charles and his family.

'Probably in gratitude that she is a girl, no doubt,' Douglas remarked. 'He'll have to send boots, next time.'

May had already factored in a next time but she would give herself at least two years grace before that.

There had even been a pretty card, of a mother smiling at a

tiny baby, from William, signed, 'Your faithful friend.' Good, she thought, even he does not suspect and he still wants to be my friend.

She was relieved and pleased that Douglas had accepted the baby, even though it was a girl, but soon felt a prick of jealousy at his obsession with the child. All he seemed to want to talk about was the latest thing **his** daughter had done.

In moments of jealousy she was tempted to tell him the truth, but sanity prevailed. He would get over it. She would still be his most precious possession and, in time, when she produced the longed for son, little Flora would become just another member of the household. She felt sympathy for the baby who would lose her favoured status just as she was becoming old enough to understand it. Let her have her year or two of celebrity while she could.

Her only worry was that William might move away or, God forbid, marry. She had had a moments panic when he had informed her that he was enlisting to fight in the war raging in Europe, but fate had intervened. He was declared medically unfit, having weak lungs. To forestall any chance of him moving away from Brisbane she made sure that Douglas recommended him to all his friends. But William did not need Douglas' endorsement. In his own, quiet way, William was making a name for himself in the world of architecture.

The orderly world of British Imperialism was changing. The wireless that Douglas had brought May as a wedding present now became their window onto the world. He had thought of it as an indulgence and had had it installed in her little sitting room. Now it took pride of place in his lounge and, at midday and at six p.m. everything stopped as the whole household listened to the ever more devastating accounts of the wars raging in Europe and Africa.

Foreign correspondents became household names as they vividly described the retreats, the bombings, the surrenders, culminating in evacuation at Dunkirk Soon it seemed that Britain stood alone against the might of Germany and Italy. The news that H.M.A.S. Sydney had sunk an Italian Cruiser was one item that raised patriotic morale but everybody agreed that there was not going to be any quick victory. In far away Australia, they listened with pride to the defiant speech of Winston Churchill, *"we will never surrender "* but feared that the world, as they knew it, might be gone forever.

Douglas had a large map of the world installed in his private study where he followed the course of the war, marking its progress with red and black pins. All too often the black pins seemed to be outnumbering the red.

With so many enlisting, and well-paid, government jobs available, it became almost impossible to retain domestic staff. Jessica was stretched to the limit with only one, long time maid to assist.

Douglas became aware of the situation when he could not replace his gardener and odd jobs man. He rectified this by employing an Italian from an internment camp. Beppi and Rosa Juliano had been in Australia for more than twenty years but had never bothered to become naturalized so, when Italy had entered the war, Beppi was placed in an internment camp. Douglas had no trouble in having him assigned to his care, and, to Jessica's relief, his wife Rosa came too, as cook.

Edna, the former cook, had been used to a kitchen maid and a small kitchen staff. As each girl had left, her workload became harder and harder. Though she still felt loyalty to the family she wished to leave and was pleased when she had a legitimate reason to resign.

Her son-in-law had enlisted and was with the Fifth Division, leaving his wife, Nell, with two small children. She begged her mother to come and live with her and help care for the children while she joined the workforce.

'It will be a marvellous opportunity Mum. We can live on the money I earn and bank all Jack's pay. When he returns we will have a nice little nest egg to make a better life for the kids.'

And a start for you if he does not return, her mother thought.

So Rosa and Beppi were welcomed by all the family. The old, detached kitchen had become a storeroom. This was converted into a two roomed flat and the new couple set up home there. Soon, strange vegetables and herbs appeared in the vegetable garden and delicious, new smells emerged from the kitchen.

Jessica was at first suspicious of inviting enemy aliens into the house but quickly came to appreciate Rosa's competence and soon learnt that she could leave the kitchen in safe hands. Beppi proved to be multi-skilled and was soon indispensable around the house. 'They are such nice people. What a pity they have such poor leaders,' Jessica thought.

Douglas would have agreed with her. Mussolini didn't know what he was up against. He knew about desert campaigns. He had fought to suppress the Senussi who were now loyal members of the empire. The Italians would find them a wirily enemy and the British would never surrender Egypt. The Suez was much too important.

He was the authority on this theatre of war among his friends. For once he did not feel inferior to those who had fought in Gallipoli and the Western Front. He had done his part too.

They all rejoiced at the rapid successes of the Tenth Army and made jokes about the number of prisoners taken.

'I heard it from a good authority that whole battalions just wait around until they can find someone to surrender to. They didn't want this war any more than we did,' Jock Mackenzie informed them.

CHAPTER 18

ADELAIDE

Joel and I keep in contact by phone, which pleases my mother, though I had to tell the odd lie about friends and homework if the call came when Flora was around. She was not a fan of mobiles.

'In my day it was enough for families to have one phone, situated in the hall for privacy. The only people who needed multiple phones were Starting Price Bookmakers.'

On Saturday he rang early.

'Are you doing anything this morning?'

'Nothing special. Why?'

'We are never going to get to the bottom of all this without a bit of help, so if you meet me at the State Library, just before ten, we might find out a bit more about your family.'

'See you there, then.' I hung up quickly before I said something to embarrass myself.

I have a date with Joel! But it is not the usual type of date. I am going to meet him at the State Library. Of course it has to do with the family feud but maybe, maybe, it will lead to something else. At least it's a start and it means he has not given up on partnering me to the formal.

When we met in front of Parliament House he gave me a peck

on the cheek, *I suppose that all you can expect in public. Should I take encourage from it?*

'I found out that you can access Ancestry dot. com. at the library for free,' he told me. 'You can't run off any documents but you can look at them, so I thought we could look up your famous grandfather, see what we can find. I've booked us in for ten.'

'At least we might find out who my grandmother was. Do you think she was the one who was killed? Maybe that's why there are no photos of her?' I gave him my most seductive look, 'and afterwards?'

'If it doesn't take too long we could have a coffee, but I've got footy at one.'

Well, that's something, I suppose.

The library assistant had everything set up, so it didn't take us long to find the right Douglas Henderson. I learnt, for the first time, that his second name was Ewan and that in 1938 he married May Edith Swan. They had one daughter, my esteemed grandmother, Flora Jean born in 1940.

'Wait a minute,' Joel said, 'Grandad's mother was called May! Wow! Could she be the same woman? Could this be what the row was about?'

We immediately hunted up Joel's Grandad, Robert, and got pretty excited when we found that his mother was indeed May Swan. The librarian even frowned at us, so we tried to behave ourselves but, when we investigated a little further we found that, although William Forbes was indeed registered as his father, there was no record of a marriage.

'This gets betterer and betterer. Way to go.' Joel shouted, punching the air and I got the giggles. *Perhaps co-habiting runs in the family.*

The librarian must have stood up from her seat and headed towards us but we were too caught up with our discoveries to notice.

I suddenly stopped laughing as the full implications of our discovery sank in. 'Joel, if May was mother to both of them that means we are related.'

'So we are.' Joel thought for a moment. 'A great grandmother? Sooo, that would make us kissing cousins.'

And he did, and not just a peck either.

'This behaviour is not permitted in this place. I must ask you both to leave.'

The librarian had arrived just as the kiss was becoming interesting. We apologised as best we could, trying not to laugh but, as soon as we got into the foyer, we collapsed into uncontrollable mirth.

'Kicked out of the library for conduct unbecoming,' Joel explained to those around, between peals of laughter then almost collapsed on the floor. We were still roaring our heads off when we got outside. I don't think I have ever laughed so much in all my life. My ribs were aching and my mouth dry, but I couldn't stop. We were like a couple of drunks. It's a wonder we weren't arrested.

Eventually it wore off, but we couldn't look at each other without beginning again.

'Do you think we can stop long enough to go for a coffee?' Joel asked.

'Let's try.'

We crossed the road, went to the food hall and managed to order cappuccinos and bagels, but had to keep the conversation to, "pass the sugar, topics" because we didn't want to be thrown out of there, too.

'Shit.'

Joel must have looked at the wall clock for he suddenly stood up. 'Sorry, I've got to go. I'll get murdered if I don't turn up. I can't risk that just when life is becoming interesting. When can I see you?'

'If we're still on, there's a practice at the Town Hall, Tuesday at five'

'Be there, with bells on. See ya,' and he gave me a gentle brotherly kiss on the top of my head and hurried off.

It was only then I released the breath I had been holding, waiting for an answer to my question.

'Yes!' I punched the air, then realising where I was, put my head down and contemplated the crumbs on my plate until I felt able to face the diners. I wanted to go up to each table and spread the good news that I was in love. I walked home, it wasn't that far, and it gave me time to get a grip.

It's funny when you're feeling happy how everything seems to be a little brighter. This must be what all those soppy love songs and poems are about and, if that is so, am I in for the big let down that so often seems to follow?

I've never been a big reader of romantic fiction. Most of the ones I have read were on the study syllabus and I hardly ever sympathised with the heroine. I felt like saying, "so what, get a life." Now I'm in the middle of a family drama and a grand romance. It could have been written by Emily Bronte.

Part of me wants to cry, "help, get me out of here," but most of me likes the feeling so much that I want it to last forever

'I'm home,' I called, to anyone who might be interested. I went straight to my room and threw myself on my bed. I couldn't remember ever feeling so happy in my whole life. Whether it was because of Joel or just the feeling itself I wasn't sure? But I had no intentions of analysing that feeling now. It was too precious.

CHAPTER 19

1942 / 1943

Until December "the war", while a reality in everyone's minds, had nevertheless not been seen as a personal threat, unless one had a family member serving in the Forces.

Australians at home had followed the advance of the Axis forces through maps appearing in the daily newspapers, heard the harrowing stories of Nazi brutality on the radio and watched newsreel footage of the destruction caused by the bombing of English cities. The only good news seemed to be coming from Africa where the Italians were on the run. But it was all "over there".

Each month of '41 seemed to bring more distressing news. A general called Rommel took over command of the defence of Tripoli and forced the Allied troops into a full-scale retreat. Douglas followed the daily reports on the North African campaign with special interest as it brought back memories of his own war. When the Sixth division halted the German Africa Corps at Tobruk he felt a personal pride. He would have given most of his wealth if only he could have been one of the "Rats of Tobruk."

On the 7th October he was dismayed that the conservative

government lost the election and the country was now being ruled by Labor.

'It is disastrous to change horses in mid-stream.' he declared. 'Only worse events will follow.'

His prediction seemed to have come true when the news of the sinking of the Sydney, practically on the doorstep, became known. 'Even distance will not save us if the Hun wins.' he lamented.

Then, overnight their world, as they knew it, changed forever. On the 7th December, Japanese bombers attacked a place called Pearl Harbour, destroying much of the United States Pacific fleet. Suddenly there was a new ally, and a frightening, new enemy. An Asiatic country, known mainly for its cheap, inferior exports, had challenged the might of America. If anyone had thought they would be easily beaten, the speed of their victories proved that they were indeed a formidable foe. It was obvious that Japan was intent on dominating all of Asia and the Pacific. Suddenly the safety of distance was gone.

War was on the doorstep.

Fear turned to despair as Thailand, Malaya, Philippines, Hong Kong, Guam, Nauru, Wake and Ocean Island were attacked simultaneously. It brought home to all the reality that Japan was capable of taking on the might of the Allies and succeeding. Suddenly the war became personal.

The fall of Singapore in February, with the capture of most of the Australian Eighth Division meant that Australia was defenceless. Four days later bombs were dropped on Darwin.

The speed of the advances, the killing or capture of so many Australian fighting men and the arrival of Dutch refugees from Java all proved that Australia was no longer safe.

In 1938, when a new Highland Battalion, the 61st, had been raised in Queensland, Douglas had offered his services, only to be told that men over forty were not to be enlisted. He was highly offended by this so, when war had been declared, he felt no great call to duty.

However, with the entry of Japan into the conflict, he placed himself at the disposal of his country. He was given his old commission and a position in the Ministry of Food and Distribution. His first job was to take a census of all livestock in the Darling Downs. Food was an essential component of war and, in the event of imminent invasion, all livestock was to be moved south or destroyed.

Douglas knew that he could be sent anywhere so he thought it expedient for May and Flora to leave Brisbane.

'I'm afraid, my dear, that I am no longer my own man. I could be sent anywhere, at any time, therefore I think it sensible that you and Flora, and your mother too, should leave Brisbane.'

May had been so engrossed with her new role of mother that much of world politics had passed her by but with the entry of Japan she suddenly realised that 'the war' was not something far away that she only had to think of occasionally when some new defeat was reported. Now it was coming closer and could affect her too. She was truly frightened about the advancing enemy. Darwin is not that far from Brisbane, she thought.

She was delighted to be sent south, out of danger's way, but feigned disappointment.

'Douglas, how could I leave you at such a time, but if you think it necessary, I will move to Sydney.'

'Don't be stupid, woman. Sydney will be even more

dangerous than Brisbane. I expect to hear any day now that they have bombed it. No, you must go to Lochaber.'

'Lochaber?' May was horrified. She remembered her one short visit there soon after her marriage. 'I could never live there. It is too far away.'

'That's the whole point. The Japanese aren't interested in farming. They're into manufacturing. It will be the big cities they're after. Not that they will ever get this far, mind you, the Americans will stop them. But they have planes, lots of planes. So they'll be dropping bombs on the cities, just like the Germans do. Sydney will be their main target. You will be safe at Lochaber. They couldn't even find it, let alone waste a bomb on it. Cheer up. There will be lots to do there. You may even learn to ride a horse and muster sheep.'

May shuddered. Unlike some of her friends she had never taken to horses. She would have to find some reason to stay.

Although Douglas had assured May that the Japanese would never land in Australia, his private nightmare was that, while he was away doing his duty, vile Japanese soldiers would arrive in Brisbane and run riot among unprotected females. He had visions of May and even his baby daughter being ravished by the heathen, yellow devils. He made preparations for such an event.

'Jess, I have always been able to rely on you to do the sensible thing. I am sure you will never have to use them but, in wartime, one must always take into account a worst-case scenario. You know that the Japanese are totally uncivilised and the sight of white women will send them into a frenzy of debauchery. To save you all from this I have acquired these pills. Before they enter this house you must give one to May and one to Flora.

There is one for you also, as age will be no barrier.'

Jessica swallowed the unintended insult. 'That is very thoughtful of you, Douglas, but I have more faith in our fighting forces than you. We will not be invaded. But to ease your mind I will keep these safe.'

She accepted the little box of pills and hid them in her room. She wondered if, should there be an actual invasion, she would have the courage to kill her daughter and granddaughter.

When rationing began, in July 42, Douglas' duties were also to investigate any breaches of the act. Black marketeers were second only to Axis spies.

May was never banished to Lochaber. Fate took a hand and a new role was found for her. The U.S. army headquarters were established in Brisbane. Victoria Park was requisitioned. Numerous prefabricated huts and barracks dotted the parkland where hundreds of American servicemen lived and worked at the camp while Australian civilians were employed there

In July, General Douglas MacArthur, Chief of Staff of the American Army, decided to establish his base in Brisbane. The population of Brisbane almost doubled, thanks to an influx of young American servicemen. A marine base was stationed in New Farm.

MacArthur and all his military personnel moved north, and important visitors, including celebrities of stage and screen, were coming and going. Even in wartime such people had to be entertained. *Inverrigan* opened its doors and May shone in her role as hostess. The MacArthurs came, Premier Cooper came, Brigadiers and Generals came, even international stars like Bob Hope and Connie Francis came to *Inverrigan*. Whether it was hosting dinners for visiting dignitaries in the big hall, garden parties in the gardens, fund raising dances, or acting as escort to colonels and brigadiers when they attended official entertainments, she was in her element.

Her new role took up so much of her time that little baby Flora became Jessica's responsibility, a role that she was only too willing to fill.

Douglas was proud of his wife. He basked in the compliments paid to her, taking them as a reflection of his own importance. She was much too valuable to be sent up country.

As 1942 proceeded more and more United States Military units arrived in Australia in greater numbers before being deployed to New Guinea. Brisbane's population more than doubled almost overnight.

In time this led to arguments and fights between Australian and American servicemen. "Over paid, over sexed and over here" was an oft repeated complaint.

There were many clashes and any number of reasons for them but it all culminated in what would come to be known as *The Battle of Brisbane* where, for two nights, the 26th and 27th of November spasmodic fighting broke out throughout the city. There were many casualties on both sides but eventually an uneasy peace settled on the city as both sides got on with fighting the real enemy, the Japanese.

At *Inverrigan* the whole episode was looked on with bemusement. Douglas, having been a fighting man during the First World War understood how men, waiting to be sent to "death or glory" would sometimes let off steam. But May found it most confusing.

'Every American I have ever met,' she declared, 'has been a perfect gentleman.'

The only American serviceman who had been entertained at *Inverrigan* had been officers of the higher order and on their best behaviour, so hers may have been a biased view.

May enjoyed the war years. If it had not been for the constant, nagging fear that one day the country would be invaded, she would have thought of them as the best years of her life.

The bombings of Darwin, Broome and Derby and the submarine attack in Sydney brought the threat very close, but after victories of the Coral Sea and at Kokoda the tide of war began to turn and life seemed to become one long party. May knew that not everyone was happy with so many handsome, cashed up young men walking the streets of Brisbane but they brought a vitality to a small city that had been considered a backwater by its southern neighbours.

May thought all the officers who frequented her house sophisticated and romantic. They had beautiful manners and seemed to understand women so much better than the men she had known. They brought a new energy to the sleepy city and the latest music and dance steps to entertain both young and old. She was in love with everything American.

It was only Jessica's close supervision, as well as her memory of Douglas' warning in New Zealand, that saved her from getting herself into a serious predicament. She was at heart a romantic and it was not sex but romance she sought.

CHAPTER 20

1944

By 1944, when the threat of invasion had ceased, May felt that it was time to make a little brother for Flora. She was pleased with herself that she had not given way to the temptation to find an American father for the child. Better to fish in the same pond she reasoned. That way there would be a similarity between both children.

During her glory days of entertaining she had sadly neglected William Forbes. She would have to rectify that position as quickly as possible.

William's firm had gained several government contracts during the war years and he was now an established and respected architect and, with the prospect of a massive rebuilding program when the war was over, it was not difficult to find a reason to have him invited to some of her social evenings. She always introduced him as her oldest friend and was reassured to see that he was as much in love with her as he had been on her eighteenth birthday. She would be able to rely on him.

William found it hard to recognise the May he had known, in the successful hostess who managed to mix so naturally with older successful and famous people.

How could he have ever thought that she would have been happy with such a dull, uninteresting person as himself?

But in a moment when they found themselves alone she gave him a sad sigh.

'Willie,' she whispered, 'Do not believe what you see. These parties, they are only to keep up morale, my war effort. I would much sooner be sitting in a corner talking honestly to a good friend. You are still my friend, aren't you?'

'Of course I am, May. I will always be your friend.'

He wished he could tell her how much more he wanted to be, but at least he could give her friendship.

She dropped hints to him that she was really miserable despite all the gayety, that she felt alone amid the throng. He was her only true friend, the only one who really understood her, the one person who could see the real May amid all the glamour.

She knew it would not be long before he would be visiting her in the summerhouse.

Another person who was enjoying the war was Gerard Reid. Thanks to the influence of some of his indebted customers, he had evaded the call up by gaining important government employment.

He had found, among the Americans, men after his own heart. Wartime meant scarcity and scarcity meant people willing to pay for rationed and scarce goods. The Americans were able to provide them, and he was able to look after their distribution. Together they were making big money.

Though still living at home Gerard could come and go as he pleased. He had a nippy little Austin Bantam and a good supply of petrol, thanks to his new friends. He was soon known as the "go-to man" by anyone in Brisbane and beyond who needed booze, cigarettes, petrol or nylons.

Some privately speculated about his affluence, but his family was held in such high regard, and those who had been contributing to his lifestyle were too conscious of their own vulnerability, for anyone to seriously question it. Still there were those who would not have shed a tear had he suddenly driven off a cliff.

Gerard had never quite got over the fact that May had slipped through his fingers. As a neighbour and son of Douglas' best friend, he was often included in invitations at *Inverrigan*. He had kept a weather eye on May, expecting her to make a mistake with one of the many charming Americans who came and went but, though she flirted outrageously, he was amazed at her ability to keep any situation under control. He wondered how one so young could have acquired such poise.

May began her plans to once again convince Douglas that he would be the father of the child she hoped to conceive.

'Douglas, the war is really going well, isn't it?'

'Of course it is, May. Only a matter of time. They'll take Rome any day now.'

'But the Japanese?'

'All but finished. MacArthur is wiping them up, one island at a time, and we've got them on the run in New Guinea. They can't invade us now, can't even bomb us. Don't know why they don't just give up and surrender. You can relax, my dear.'

May gave him a coy look. 'Then Douglas, do you think it might be time to try for a little boy?'

'Do you mean . . .?'

'Yes.' She gave him a beaming smile. 'I've already bought some more of those horrible herbs and I believe oysters are getting easier to buy these days.'

Douglas had a twinkle in his eye as he replied, 'Then, my dear, It's up to me. I will do my duty and I can assure you it will be a pleasure.'

What with constant travel related to his war work, May's constant engagement at home and advancing age, there had not been a lot of action on the home front of late. Making a baby would be a happy distraction.

'It's about time Flora had a bit of competition. The little minx thinks she rules the place.'

'And who's to blame? You and Mother do spoil her so.'

'I suppose I do. But she is so easy to spoil.'

May made a great display of drinking the horrible herbs and shuddering as she ate her oysters and Douglas did his duty whenever he was home. Meanwhile, William became a constant guest each time she held one of her fund raising dinners.

William was tormented every time he went to an evening at *Inverrigan.* Occasional meetings in daytime were bearable. In fact they reassured him that May was coping with her situation, but evenings were different. Not only did he suffer pangs of jealousy watching her dance and flirt with sophisticated, handsome Americans in uniform, but they brought back memories of that mad time before May had brought him to his senses. To continue the relationship would have brought ruin on them both. He had to acknowledge that now. He always believed that, to reward her for her strength, fate had blessed with her daughter.

Sometimes seeing her became too hard for him. He was afraid that one night he would forget himself and declare his love in public. He promised himself that he would find an excuse not to attend, he would leave Brisbane and start again, he tried again to enlisting. He even started dating other women. But one summons and his best intentions were undone. She was his one and only love. All that was left to him was to throw himself into his work and be there, in case she ever needed him.

Tonight was such a night. He had endured it for over an hour. It was time to go. He walked towards May intending to thank her for a lovely evening then make his way home.

As if she had read his thoughts May came towards him, asking if he would like another drink, then whispered, 'Willie, I must see you. Meet me in the summerhouse when all these people have gone.'

He could only manage a nod.

May slipped seamlessly back into her hostess mode, leaving him breathless, heart pounding and weak at the knees.

William didn't even bother to excuse himself but wandered down the path, through the trees. Because of the blackout there were no lights to guide him but he had no difficulty finding his way to the building where he had known those few weeks of ecstasy. He had been faithful to his vow, but he knew that he would not be strong enough to restrain himself if he were alone with her again.

In time he heard, in the distance, the sounds of farewell, last minute shouted messages, slamming car doors, crunching gravel, then silence. He waited and waited, but she did not come.

What had detained her? Had Douglas returned? Had he misinterpreted what she had said? He was just about to give up when she finally appeared.

'Oh, Willie, Willie darling, you waited.' She threw herself into his arms. They kissed and caressed with such passion and urgency that no power on earth could have stopped the coupling. They didn't even make it to the lounge.

May really enjoyed the sex this time. She realised she had been missing the enthusiasm Douglas had displayed in the early days of their marriage. These days he was often away and at home seemed to perform as if it was a duty.

The vigour of the younger man so pleased her that she found it hard to play the penitent wife, but play it she did. William went away convinced that he had once again seduced her when all she had wanted was the comfort of his arms.

May had opened the door again. Willie still loved her as much as ever. There would be no problem with him but it would take all her skill of persuasion to be sure of success. It would not be so easy to arrange these trysts this time. Douglas' absences were not predictable or extended. He was at the bidding of his country. He would be gone, a day here, a week there and often with little warning.

Also, there were now many demands on her own time. She would have to play her game carefully. She could not just ring Willie up whenever her husband was absent and she feared that, if his conscience began to worry him, Willie might stop coming to her events.

She would have to walk a fine line between lonely maiden

and repentant wife. She recognised that William would only be able to keep his love for her a secret for so long. She would have to play her game long enough to begin another pregnancy then find a way to break their relationship. She would really miss him but twice was enough. It would be her life if Douglas ever found out.

A week or so later, while Douglas was away, a dance was held at *Inverrigan* for important locals and some of the marine officers stationed nearby. Several of Douglas' old friends stood, glass in hand, watching the younger generation gyrating around the floor, to loud, unfamiliar music. They agreed that it had a certain rhythm but were bewildered that anyone could call it dance music.

'It's called "The Jitterbug" or something,' Colin Redmann informed his friends. He had grandchildren who kept him abreast with the latest fashions.

'Well named. It looks as if they're got more than bugs in their trousers,' his companion observed. 'Look what that fellow is doing to that girl, throwing her up, swinging her around. My god, he's dragging her between his legs now. There should be a law against it.'

'I don't know,' Colin replied, 'they seem to be enjoying it and it does provide a pleasant view for observers. Anyway, there's May Henderson taking lessons. Douglas must think it is O.K.'

William watched, mesmerized, as May listened intently to a particularly handsome Marine Captain and followed his instructions as she navigated the dance steps. He felt a stab of jealousy. He would have liked to be so intimate with her in public.

Thinking himself unobserved, he relaxed. His eyes feasted on the laughing, animated creature. He knew that others envied the American who twirled and twisted her young body, but only he knew this was the public May, the welcomer, the hostess, the wife of Douglas Henderson. If only they knew the other May and the secret passion, reserved for him alone. Just when he had resigned himself to a loveless life, she had beckoned him again. This time would be different. Somehow, someway they had to make a life together.

But there was also the watcher who watched the watcher, Gerard Reid. He was good at reading body language, secret signs, and here was raw emotion, if he had ever seen it. The poor fool. Still carrying a torch for her. So that's why he has never had a girlfriend.

Gerald sidled up and whispered in William's ear, 'You can look, but it won't do you any good now, man. Should have taken your chances while you could.'

William was jolted out of his dream. 'What do you mean?"

'She was never in the market for the likes of you and me. Sold herself to the old man, but I bet she's giving him value for money.'

A volcano of anger erupted inside William. Now the most peaceful of men, he had learnt to hold his own in the streets of Glasgow when a boy. His fury exploded into power in his right arm. It shot along it and his fist, when it came in contact with Gerard's jaw, was solid rock.

Gerard was taken off guard, but even if he had been forewarned, he could not have absorbed the punch. He staggered back, fell against a drink-table and landed unceremoniously on the floor.

In that moment everything stopped but William, still in the grip of anger, stood over Gerard and spoke loudly enough for all to hear.

'If I ever hear you speak a disparaging word against that woman again, I will kill you.'

'Willie!'

His anger subsided as, looking up, he saw the expression of horror on May's face. What had he done?

He looked at Gerard, sitting on the floor amid the broken shreds of glass, rubbing his chin, then back at May.

'Sorry.' He turned and almost ran from the room.

Only Gerard saw the look that had passed between the two young people.

Well I never, he thought, who'd have guessed it was little Willie Forbes?'

People rushed forward to help him

'Are you all right?'

'What brought that on?'

'That lad's got a temper'

'Do you want to charge him?'

Gerard held up a hand and was helped up, trying to regain a little comportment. 'It was nothing. Men's business. Sorry to have disturbed you. Please go on.'

He accepted the offers of sympathy, assuring everyone that only his dignity had been hurt. Waiting just long enough to show his departure was not a retreat, he left. He had some very serious thinking to do. He had always had his suspicions about who actually had been Flora's father. He now believed he had the answer to his question. But at present it was only a hunch. He needed evidence.

Now that he knew who the quarry was he would hunt him down. He was sure that it would not take long to get proof. The hunt would be exhilarating and success would bring its own rewards.

CHAPTER 21

When Ewan Henderson had first moved to Brunswick St. New Farm, it had consisted of large, ornate homes, set on small estates, and shady, tree lined streets. By the time Douglas became master of *Inverrigan* its desirability as a convenient commuter suburb made it a much sought-after residential area.

This development had been the main motivation for Douglas becoming interested in local politics, but he found he was often a lone voice. More and more people were moving to New Farm, which made subdivision lucrative. People he felt he could rely on to hold the line were relinquishing their acres. Instead of the well-spaced homes of former days, most had become infested with apartments. Granted they were worthy buildings in themselves and the occupants were of the professional class, but they were so close, so intrusive. He wondered how a man could breathe with his neighbours living all around him.

He had become disillusioned with the intrigue of local politics. It made him feel that he was a very little cog in a big wheel. It offended him.

The war had changed all that. His war work gave him, not just power, but prestige. He was safeguarding the food of the nation and ensuring that a steady supply of essentials reached the allies fighting to free the world from the hated Hun and Nips.

Still there were times when his duty brought real pain and tonight was one such time. If Albert Reid had not been one of his oldest friends he would have had no compunction in following up on the information he had been given. But Albert was a respected citizen, a fellow soldier and one of the original habitants of New Farm. Surely he deserved a warning before news like this became public.

Though it was late when he called, Albert welcomed the visit. 'Douglas, long time no see. This war is certainly keeping us busy.'

Douglas laughed. 'I don't know what you've been up to but I've been travelling the length and breadth of the state and beyond. I keep a case permanently packed. All I can say is thank God for the railways. Still, the tide has turned. It is only a matter of time now.'

The two men chatted as they walked into the study. Albert poured two whiskeys into glasses on the sideboard without even asking. It was not until they

were settled in the Chesterfield armchairs that Douglas came to the reason for his visit.

'I am afraid, Albert, that this is not a social call.'

'Has it to do with Gerard?'

This response surprised him. 'Yes! Why do you ask?'

'I have known for years that my son is not the man I would have wished him to be. I am not surprised to hear that he has been up to things I would rather know nothing about. For some time I have heard the odd rumour but have been too ashamed to investigate.'

'What have you heard about him?'

'Rumours about his gambling, the company he keeps, the

way he always seems to have money though I have no idea how he earns it. He never seems to be at the office. Just does enough work to justify his salary. You may have heard about the scrap he had with that young man, Forbes, at your home. Seems Gerard was making disparaging remarks about some young woman and Forbes called him out. Floored him, I am told. At least Gerard had the sense not to take it any further. I dread the day when I will see his name splashed across the pages of one of those scandal rags. Even his mother is quietly worried, though she will not hear a word against him.'

Albert put down his glass on the small table near his chair, turned to Douglas and opened his hands, appealing to his friend. 'I have seen people look at me and I know they are thinking, *could the rumours be true?'*

'I do not listen to rumours, Albert, though the goings on in some quarters would leave a number of our noble citizens open to criticism. No, I am speaking of national security.'

'You don't mean . . .?'

Douglas, seeing the look of horror on his friend's face quickly reassured him. 'No, I do not mean spying or anything like that, but the offence is just as serious. No, I have been investigating a black market racket for some time. The Americans opened our eyes to it. Gerard's name has surfaced so I thought I should let you know.

'They want me to investigate, on the quiet. They do not want a scandal on their side. Not good for morale. Where it will lead to I do not know, but, as a friend, I thought I should prepare you for the publicity that will follow if he is found to be involved.' He watched the proud man crumble before his eyes.

'Douglas, my family have been upholders of British law for

centuries. There have been one or two eccentrics, but nobody, not one, has ever been charged with actually breaking the law. To have this charge – at such a time – in the middle of the greatest war – when the very way of civilized life is in danger – I tell you truly, Douglas, I wish the boy had never been born. I wish he had died at birth or as one of our gallant soldiers who died at Tobruk. Anything but this. How can I live with such a scandal?'

Douglas could find no words to console his friend. He stood and placed his hand on his friend's shoulder and patted it. Albert covered his face to hide his shame.

In time he gained some control. He rose and held out his hand. 'Thank you, Douglas, for giving me time to absorb the shock. It will give me a chance to prepare his mother. When will you begin your investigations?'

'As soon as I finish some government business I have in Ipswich. The Americans need a few days to deal with their end of the problem without creating any adverse publicity. They plan to send their men back, state side, a quick military trial and, if found guilty, probably shot.

'Of course, the information I have been given may prove to be wrong, but I will still have to investigate, and you know how rumour spreads, even if it turns out there was nothing to it. I thought you should be warned. Albert, just remember that, whatever others will say, I will not judge you and will always be proud to call myself your friend.'

Douglas was so overcome with emotion himself that he hurried out, not noticing a shadowy figure lurking in the darkened passage.

Gerard walked slowly back to his own quarters. He had been congratulating himself that he had recently more or less confirmed a suspicion he had. He had been planning to make quite a handsome profit from the knowledge, but now he would have to use it to get himself out of a nasty jam. At least he had something to bargain with. He did not think Douglas Henderson would be happy to have the story of his wife's infidelity spread around the town.

He had, at one time thought of her as a potential wife and had taken it as an insult when she seemed to have shown a preference for William. When she had become Mrs Douglas Henderson, he had put her onto his potential blackmail list, but she had become the perfect wife. He had lost interest, until Flora was born.

He had heard and believed the rumour that Douglas was incapable of producing offspring as the result of some disease he had contracted years ago during the war. If it was true then who was the father?

He had renewed his surveillance to no avail. She never seemed to overstep her social obligations, even though there had been many opportunities, with Douglas often absent and any number of eligible young Americans in and out of the house. Either the rumours had been wrong or Flora had had an immaculate conception.

Only after his altercation with William had he suspected that little Willie Forbes could be the father of the child Douglas was so proud of. It made sense. They had known each other for years and William had always been madly in love with her. But suspicions were not enough. He needed proof. He had renewed his snooping and now believed he had enough proof that

William was May's lover and more than likely the father of Flora.

With a steady income from his black market activities he had thought to use the information only as pressure to gain a few favours from May for himself. Now it could be a vital weapon in saving his skin.

How he was going to silence his father was another thing, but he would think about that after he had neutralised Douglas. Surely any man would put his son's future before his own honour?

CHAPTER 22

Gerard thought carefully about how he would use the knowledge he had to best advantage. Should he just confront Douglas with all the facts, drop a hint or two, or start embarrassing rumours?

He didn't relish confronting Douglas directly. The man might be twice his age but it was rumoured he had a fearful temper and Gerard had never won his arguments by using physical force. However, he had to get the man's attention, and quickly, or his threat would have no power. Douglas had said he would be away for a couple of days, so perhaps the best tactic would be to make the initial approach by letter.

Gerard gave more attention to the wording of the letter than to any of the essays he had written during his university days, Eventually, he felt confident that what he had written would, at least, delay Douglas' reporting long enough to give him a chance to save himself from criminal charges.

Just after eight the next evening, Gerard parked his car and walked up the gravelled drive. Now that the centre of the Pacific war had moved to the north there were fewer Americans in Brisbane and fewer events at *Inverrigan*. Tonight there was only one line of light showing through the black-out curtains on the ground floor.

He grabbed the brass knocker and knocked strongly. He heard the sound reverberating inside the house and waited. He knew Douglas was not home but still he felt fear. This could be the most important moment in his life. He must not fail. He was about to raise the knocker again when a dim light went on above his head and the door opened.

'Gerard, what a pleasant surprise.' Jessica's pleasant greeting was not reflected in her eyes. What was this young man doing on the doorstep at this time of night?

'Good evening, Mrs Swann. I'm sorry to disturb you but I was wondering if Mr Henderson were at home?'

'I am sorry Gerard, but he left this afternoon. He will be away until Saturday. If it is important I could contact him on the phone at the hotel where he will be tonight.'

'Not to worry, Mrs Swann. We thought that might be the case so I have written the message.'

'Is it from your father?'

Should he say yes or no? Best to be noncommittal.

'It is imperative that he read it as soon as he returns. You will see that he does, Mrs Swann.'

'Of course, Gerard. Do you wish to come inside? I could call May.'

'No, thank you, I'm just delivering the letter on my way to a further engagement.'

'Then I won't detain you. I hope you have a pleasant evening.'

Jessica watched as he sauntered down the drive then closed the door. In the dim light from the sitting room she turned the letter over in her hand. It looked innocent enough, but why was it hand delivered? It had no writing on the envelope. Perhaps she should inspect it then put it in a new one. She wasn't a natural snooper, but Douglas had been rather preoccupied lately and there was something about that boy that she had never liked. He didn't actually say it was from his father so it might not have anything to do with the law but it would be best to make sure.

Gerard had not intended to loiter after delivering the letter, but as he turned towards his car, he noticed lights flickering in the summerhouse. He already suspected what went on there. Perhaps he could catch them in the act.

Peering through a louver he was disappointed to see that May was alone. She sat amid a nest of cushions, reading. She looked so lovely in the flickering candlelight. She had always been a beauty. In the golden glow she was like something out of a fairy tale, a maiden waiting for her prince.

May was not expecting visitors that night. In fact she was setting the scene for her declaration to William that they must never be together again. His sperm had done its work again so now she would have to end the relationship. It would be much harder for her this time. Then she had been using William for one purpose, to make a baby. She thought of him only as a provider. She had matured since then.

This time it would be different. She had come to recognized the kindness in him, his quiet dignity and his sense of honour. Most of all she appreciated his unselfish love for her. How lucky was she to be given such true, steadfast devotion. What would her life have been if she had married him?

She knew Douglas loved her too, but on his terms. She was

still a possession. And though she did have feelings for him, she knew they were governed by fear. If he suspected infidelity for one minute he would destroy her in an instant.

Now, to please her husband, she had played with Willie's love again. She had used him and was now planning to discard him. What did that say about her? Did it make her a monster like a spider she had read of who ate its mate after procreating? But it would have to be done. She rehearsed the scene - the shock, the tears –

This time she would not accuse him of seducing her. She would confess she had been a willing partner, but nevertheless make him see that it had to stop, even though she was as unwilling as he was to end it. Perhaps she would suggest that he leave Brisbane. That way they would not be renewing the pain every time they met.

The wistful look that Gerard thought of as dreaming about a lover was, in fact, a mournful regret for all that might have been.

He had been hoping that the threat in his letter to Douglas would save his skin, but why shouldn't it get him a little pleasure as well? He moved silently to the front of the building, placed his hand on the doorknob and pressed gently.

The door opened. Maybe May was already expecting a visitor? His visit would be a surprise.

'Good evening, May'

May jumped in fright. For one fleeting moment she thought it was Douglas, here to confront she for her infidelity, but then she laughed. It was only Gerard

She stood and walked towards him. 'Gerard, you gave me a dreadful fright. What are you doing here, and at this time of night?'

'I might well ask you the same question or are you already expecting a late visitor?'

'What do you mean? Why would anyone come to a summerhouse at this time of night?'

'Why indeed? I can think of any number of reasons, a lover's tryst perhaps?' It amused him to see the colour drain from her cheeks. He moved closer. 'Come on, May. Don't be so surprised. I have known, for some time, about you and our little friend. Who'd have thought, little Willie cuckolding the great Douglas Henderson? But, don't worry, we're friends.' He moved closer still, 'and friends don't tell, friends share. It's my turn now. Surely you have a little time for an old friend?'

Gerard was really enjoying himself now. He had already felt some arousal when he first saw her by candlelight. Now the fear in her eyes inflamed the passion.

'Come on, little May. Come on and learn what a real man feels like.'

He reached out to grab her, but May was not the passive victim he had expected. She stood her ground and pushed him back. He came at her, more forcefully, but she sidestepped. He had not expected this and could not control the forward thrust. If he had fallen cleanly he would have suffered no more than a dent in his dignity, but instead caught his head on the edge of a marble stand. He fell, blood streaming from a cut just below his temple and lay lifeless on the tiled floor.

Jessica felt as if she had received a fatal blow when she read Gerard's letter. When Douglas saw it the life she had worked so hard to preserve would be gone. All her planning and scheming would come to nothing, and this time she could not think of anything she could do that would help. She must warn May at once but how could she protect Flora? Douglas really loved the child but would his love turn to hate when he learned that he had been cuckolded? He would ruin May and William, her too probably, but would he abandon the child? She must speak to May at once.

CHAPTER 23

Jessica was hurrying towards the summerhouse to tell May of the disaster about to befall them when she heard the scream. Out of the corner of her eye she caught sight of Gerard's car. Could he be in the summerhouse and what was he doing to May? She threw open the door ready to defend her daughter, but was confronted with the sight of May, ghost white, hands to her head, mouth open, eyes staring at the body of Gerard Reid.

Her mother's entry broke the spell. 'He came at me, Mother. He came at me and wanted to rape me.'

She rushed into her mother's arms and buried her face in Jessica's bosom. At first she was incoherent but eventually she began to make some sense.

'He said he knows about Willie and wanted me to have sex with him to keep silent. Mother, I've killed him Mother, but I didn't mean to. He just fell.'

Jessica held her daughter. 'Shh, shh, Darling. I know you didn't mean it. But it's done. Now pull yourself together. It's a dreadful thing to happen, but it has. We can't turn back the clock, but it is not the end of the world. We are alive and we will have to come up with a plan to keep it that way.'

May's hysteria subsided into sobs but she clung to her mother. She knew that somehow, some way, her mother would get her out of this. She had always found a way.

'But what can I do?'

'First, you must calm down. Then, go to the house and ring ... William ... yes, ring William. He is the one person we can trust. Try to tell him what happened as simply as possible. Don't confuse your message. Tell him you need him. Tell him you need him, here, immediately. Tell him to get a taxi.'

Another thought, *they must cover their tracks.*

'Tell him to get a taxi but to get out before he gets to this place, and walk the rest of the way. We don't want anyone to know he was here.'

'Why, Mother?'

'I haven't worked it all out yet. Just tell him. Make him realise how serious it is. I know he will come at once. While you are doing that I will clean up here. By the time he arrives I will have a solution.'

She put her hands on her daughter's shoulders and looked deep into her eyes.

'I know this is possibly the most terrible thing that will ever happen to you in your life but you will live through it, if you keep your head. Trust me and trust William too. We both love you and we will make sure that one day this will be no more than a horrible nightmare. Now go. And put on something warmer. You're shaking like a leaf.'

May took one more look at the body, shuddered, then ran faster than she had ever done in her life. She was still trying to get her breath when the operator asked for the number.

'What number?' Her mind was blank. She took a deep breath, trying to concentrate, then noticed William's business card pinned onto a green felt board above the phone.

She was in control by the time he answered.

'Willie, it's May. No, listen. I am going to tell you something important and I don't want you to interrupt. Something terrible has happened. I'll tell you the details when you get here.'

'No, I'm not in any danger but, please listen. You must get a taxi, at once, but get out a block from here and walk the rest of the way. I will be waiting for you just inside the gate. '

'No, no. I'm quite safe but I need you here at once. And Willie, I love you.'

She put the phone back on the hook and relaxed for the first time since Gerard had fallen. Willie was coming and he would make everything better. He was good at solving problems, and he loved her.

Another realisation hit her. She loved him too. She had said it almost without thinking but all of a sudden she knew she meant it. She loved William Forbes. She had possibly loved him for years, but the silly romances she read had given her an unrealistic version of what love was. She now realised that it had nothing to do with poetry or romantic music. It was about two people finding each other and knowing that they wanted to spend the rest of their lives together.

Why had it taken this tragedy to make her realise that dear, reliable Willie was the one person in the world that she could truly love.

May's brief phone call threw William into confusion. His thoughts were like whirlpools swirling around in his head. What had happened? Was she in danger? Was he strong enough to stand up to Douglas?

He frantically rang for a taxi.

Why hadn't I bought a car, even if petrol was hard to get?

Will I be there in time?

Where is the stupid taxi? Why isn't it here?

Though it had been a quick response, considering the availability of taxis at that time, William was outside his premises, pacing up and down the street when it arrived. The vehicle was hardly stationary before he jumped inside.

'Brunswick Street.'

'You o'right, mate?'

'Yes, yes. Just go.'

'Whereabouts in Brunswick Street.?'

William was just about to give the address when he remembered May's instruction. 'Just drive along it. I will tell you when to stop.'

As he followed instructions, the driver assessed his passenger in the rear vision mirror. The bloke was certainly het up, wasn't drunk and didn't look mental, probably not dangerous but would need watching.

William, his mind filled with scenes of mayhem and horror, came to a sudden awareness. They were in Brunswick Street. There was the Reid's house.

He punched the seat in front. 'Stop! Stop!'

He had the door open by the time the car came to a screeching stop, thrust a ten shilling note into the driver's hand and was disappearing into the darkness before the man even had time to check the meter.

'Hope you're O.K. mate,' he called after the receding figure then pocketed the money. A good profit for a ten-minute drive.

May, hiding inside the gates, grabbed William as he entered, causing his pulse to race and his blood pressure to rise.

'Willie, oh Willie, you came.' She threw her arms around him and clung to him as a shipwrecked sailor would to a rock.

'May, are you all right? What has happened? Has Douglas hurt you?'

'Silly Willie.' She snuggled into his chest. 'It's got nothing to do with Douglas. Well, it has in a way but it's not what you think.'

She disentangled herself from his arms and, taking his hand, led him to a bench under a large willow tree.

'Now you must listen very carefully because my life is in your hands.' She raised her finger to cut off his protests.

'No. The most dreadful thing in my life has happened. Gerard Reid knows about us. But that's not the really bad thing that has happened.' She stifled a little sob. *How could she tell him about the hideous corpse?*

'I was in the summerhouse tonight when he burst in, told me that he knew ... and ... Oh, Willie how can I tell you?'

She took a deep breath.

'He said he would keep quiet if I would have sex with him too.' She paused and was encouraged by William's look of outrage.

'Then he came at me ... Tried to force himself upon me ... and ... oh Willie, you must believe me ... I really, truly didn't mean it to happen, but I pushed him away ... and he fell and hit his head. Now he's lying there, dead.'

The last few words were spoken almost in a whisper as she sought comfort in his arms. The tears came again but now they were tears of relief. Willie was here and he would make everything right.

William held May close, murmuring small platitudes to comfort her. Of all the scenarios he had imagined this one had not crossed his mind. He felt inadequate. What could he say?

'You are completely innocent, May. Of course it was not your fault. When you explain ... '

'No Willie. There is no way I can explain it.'

'Of course there is. When you tell everyone that he attacked you...'

'They won't believe me. They will say I had encouraged him. Don't you know the woman is always guilty. The only time a woman is believed is if she is dead and even then there are those who will say she got no more than she deserved.'

'But when you tell them how he threatened you.'

'Oh yes. Confess to infidelity. That would really help my reputation. And anyway then I would have to face Douglas. Then he would probably kill me. No, one way or another, I will be condemned, and it was not my fault.'

She broke into uncontrollable crying. She could almost feel the noose around her neck. 'Willie, Willie, you have got to save me.'

'I will, May. I will do anything. Only tell me what to do.'

After a time the crying slowed to gentle sobs and she began to think. Her mother had said that she would come up with a plan. They must go to the summerhouse.

'Willie, we must go to the summerhouse. My mother is there. She said that she would think of a plan. Come on, quickly.' She stood, grabbed his hand and dragged him towards the building.

Jessica had tidied the place as best she could. She had wiped all signs of blood from the stand and the floor. Gerard lay where he had fallen and, apart from a gash on his head, looked, for all the world, as if he were sleeping. His was the only body in the room at rest.

She now had her emotions under control. Though she would never have planned it, Gerard's death had solved the problem of his threat. All they had to do now was to keep their heads.

'William, thank you for coming. We knew we could rely on you. May has told you, truthfully what has happened, but will anyone believe her? She will have to stand trial for murder and, if convicted, she could well hang.'

Jessica spoke slowly, making sure that William would realize the seriousness of the occasion. 'I know you are an honest, honourable man but, William, even the best among us must sometimes break the rules for the better good. Gerard is dead. That is a fact and nothing can change it.

'I have come up with what I think could be a solution. But it will depend on you. You will have to lie, or at least act out what will be a lie. Are you willing to do this for May's sake?'

'Of course. I will do anything you ask.'

'Then this is the plan. As far as I know nobody knows Gerard came here unless someone noticed his car in the driveway. That is a chance we will have to take. But even if they did it would probably be irrelevant as he did come here looking for Douglas. What I propose is that we put the body in the car and you drive it. You can drive I presume?'

William nodded his head.

'Good. Then you can drive it a long way away from here, preferably to the sea or up the river, then get out and leave it in gear. If you park on a slope the car will roll over the side. By the time the wreck is found everyone will think he has had an accident or committed suicide or something. Anything but murder. Can you do this William? Can you do this for May?'

William's answer was immediate. Of course he would. He had been ready to give his life for her. Staging an accident was nothing and he would be saving her from a terrible fate.

'Of course I will.'

CHAPTER 24

Joe Weller had been lucky to miss the First World War and too old to volunteer in the second. Jumping in and out of milk carts, as he made door-to-door deliveries, wasn't the ideal job for a forty seven year old, but it beat the hell out of dying in the desert or slogging through mud in New Guinea. He might not be the fastest milkman on the block but he was reliable and he knew his customers.

In Grange Road, soon after sunrise, he was surprised to meet William Forbes just about to enter his premises. 'Why, Mr Forbes, you're out early today?'

'Just some early business to attend to.' William fished in his pocket and extracted a few coins. "I will have half a pint today, if you will.'

Deliveries over for the day, and sitting at the kitchen table, savouring a cuppa, Joe remarked to his wife, "You know that young architect fellow who lives in Grange Road You know, the one who lives above the shops? I think he must have been out on the tiles last night.'

'Drunk, was he?'

'Nah. Chasing pussy more like it and, by the looks of him, he caught some. Exhausted he was.'

'Well, good on him. At least those Yanks, with all their money and flashy uniforms aren't getting all the girls. Though I do wonder why a fit young man like him isn't in uniform?'

'Got too many brains I'd say. Smart enough to keep well out of it.'

'That's not what you were saying when the Japs were knocking at our door.'

'Well, that was then and this is now.' He raised his cup in salute. 'Good luck to him, I say.'

The conversation passed on to other things but was later called to mind as events unfolded.

On the morning of the 22nd July the favourable headlines that had been appearing ever since the Normandy invasion were temporally replaced by a local report of a tragic accident.

FATAL ACCIDENT
AT REDCLIFFE

Sometime during the evening or in the early hours, a small car, driven by Gerard Reid, son of well-known Justice Reid, left the road somewhere near Red Cliff Point. The driver was dead when an ambulance arrived. Police have not yet ascertained the nature of the accident...

There followed a history of the Reid's and the important role they had played in Queensland history and finished with a request for any eye-witnesses.

Though there was great sympathy for the Reid family there

were a few individuals who were thanking the gods that they had been delivered from the constant fear that their secret would be discovered. It would also help their bank balances.

Reading the morning paper on his way back to Brisbane, Douglas learnt of Gerard's death. His first reaction was relief that the family would not have to go through the disgrace of a trial. Next he began to question the accident itself. The report said that police were still investigating. Was it an accident, or had Albert already spoken to the boy, who had then decided to do the decent thing and save his family from disgrace, by taking an honourable way out? Whatever the reason, his old friend would be grieving. He would have to visit him as soon as he got home.

William was disgusted with himself. He had been so overwhelmed by what he was doing that, as soon as the car had begun to roll, he had run away, as if all the devils in hell were after him. He had not bothered to stay and see that the car had gone into the sea. He had failed. The first time May had asked anything of him and he had failed her. Now there would be a further investigation and no one knew where that would end.

May was cross. Just one simple task, and Willie had messed it up. How hard was it to push a car into the sea? But whatever happened there was absolutely no way anyone could connect the accident to her.

Jessica was disappointed that her plan hadn't worked as well as she hoped but at least it would have nothing to do with them. May was safe.

Four days later, when it was reported that the death was now being regarded as murder, Gerard's former victims began to fear again. Each knew that they, personally, were not responsible, but feared that, if police began to make further enquiries, like checking deposits in Gerard's bank account for instance, their names might surface and their secrets revealed. They were anxious that the perpetrator be found as quickly as possible, before further investigation might reveal Gerard's murky businesses.

The suggestion of foul play prompted the memories of several people.

A taxi driver remembered the agitated passenger he had driven to Brunswick Street that night and felt he should report it.

'It probably had nothing to do with the accident, but the young man was certainly worked up about something and I did drop him off just outside Justice Reid's home.'

A visitor, who had been at *Inverrigan* on the night William had come to blows with Gerard, remembered the threat and felt it important that he should report it.

This was the first time that William's name had come to the notice of police. It was a slim lead but one that, nevertheless, had to be followed up. He was asked to come to Roma St. to help them with enquiries.

The request worried William. How had his name come up? He was relieved when he realised that the inquiry was about the argument he had had weeks before.

'Mr Forbes, did you, on an evening in late June, have an altercation with Mr Gerard Reid?'

'I could not give you the exact date, but it would have been about that time.'

'And what was the altercation about?'

'He made a remark that offended me.'

'And you responded by punching him, causing him to fall?'

'Yes. I am not proud of losing my temper like that, but yes, I did hit him.'

The detective could see no signs of fear in William as he answered the questions. Would the next question shake his composure?

'And did you say, 'If I ever hear you say anything about that woman again, I will kill you.'

'I do not know if those were my exact words, but the meaning is about right.'

'Did you mean them as a threat?'

'I did at the time. Yes, I think I did.'

'And what was the name of the woman?'

'I would prefer not to answer that question.'

'Right, then how about this?' He paused, to give his words a stronger emphasis. 'Did you, at a later date, carry out that threat. Did you kill Gerard Reid?'

'No. I did not.' William said it with such conviction that the detective was inclined to believe him. However these were early days. Plenty of time to gather more evidence. William Forbes wasn't going anywhere.

Unfortunately, for William, a reporter for the Telegraph, in the building at the time, recognised him. He began making discreet enquiries as to why he was there and soon William's name was being whispered in public places. Others, remembering unusual events, felt it their civic duty to pass on this knowledge.

Joe Weller, at the prompting of his wife, told of the early morning incident on the day the car had been discovered. He was reluctant, but admitted that he had encounter William, very early in the morning, in a dishevelled state. 'He looked a bit like someone who had been for an early morning run, but he was in a suit.'

The taxi driver was recalled. He was shown a photo of William. He was not sure, but thought it similar to the man who had been in his taxi.

What none of these witnesses knew was that the pathologist had already discovered that, from the position in which he was found, the blow to Gerald's head could not have happened in the car. The constable who had first attended had stated that there was no blood in the car, and Gerald had died, not from a blow to the head, but from asphyxiation.

The next time William was called to Roma Street it was not for a friendly chat. He was questioned for several hours but steadfastly denied his guilt. He answered any question that did not implicate May but refused to give a satisfactory answer for what he had been doing in Brunswick Street or why he was seen outside his own establishment early next morning in a dishevelled condition.

He was detained and charged with the murder of Gerard Reid.

CHAPTER 25

Douglas was in the habit of reading the morning paper at the breakfast table

'Good God! I don't believe it.'

'What don't you believe, Douglas?'

He hesitated. May had been very despondent lately. He had been indulgent, hoping that it might be an early sign that the Chinese medicine was working. Would this news upset her? Still whether he told her or not, she would soon hear about it.

'Your friend William. It says here that he has been charged with the murder of young Reid. Well, it says he is "helping police with their enquiries," which is the newspaper's way of saying he has been charged. I can't imagine it myself. Such a quiet, well behaved young man.'

Then, thinking of what he already knew about Gerard, 'but who knows what anyone gets up to these days. Must be the war or something. Old standards are disappearing all the time. Goodness knows what the new world we are fighting for is going to be like. Hitler has a lot to answer for.'

Douglas paused and noticed, for the first time, the effect the news had had on his wife. 'May! May! Are you all right? Jess,' he shouted. 'Jess. I need you. It's May. I think she's going to faint or something. She's gone as white as a sheet.'

Jessica, who always seemed to be close when she was needed, hurried into the breakfast room, took one look at her daughter and put a protective arm around her.

'Darling, what is it? Do you want a drink of water?' May shook her head. 'Do you want to lie down?' As she said this she helped her daughter to her feet and began guiding her from the room.

Douglas stood, feeling helpless, 'Is she ill? What can I do? Should I call Rivers?'

'No, just stay. All she needs is a little rest. I will help her to her room.'

Douglas brightened up. "You don't mean…?'

'I don't mean anything, Douglas. Go back to your breakfast. Please don't make a fuss.'

The suggestion that he was "making a fuss" shocked Douglas. I'm behaving like an old woman, he thought. Better leave it to Jess. She will sort it out. If there is any news, I'll hear about it soon enough.

He sat down again and picked up the newspaper but his mind was not on the words his eyes were seeing. He loved his daughter dearly but had still longed for the son. Could it be happening after all?

As soon as they were out of hearing, Jessica quizzed her daughter.

'May, what is the matter with you? Are you ill?'

May came out of her spell. She could still breathe, but for how long, she wondered.

'Mother, it's Willie. It said in the paper he has been arrested. They will find out what I have done. Mother I'm going to be hanged for murder. Nobody will believe it was an accident.' She had buried her head in her mother's shoulder and was crying hysterically.

Jessica held her close, shhing her, trying to calm the shaking. 'It will be all right, darling. It will be all right.' Jessica was frightened too, but she knew someone had to keep her head. Everything wasn't lost. William was loyal and he would not say anything to hurt May. There was no way anyone could connect him with what had happened that night. It was all probably a big mistake, the police clutching at straws. She would get her hysterical daughter out of sight and read the news article herself. Then she could plan what to do.

Alone in his cell William contemplated his future. It had all seemed so simple when Jessica had made her plan. How were they to know that small incidents, when added together, would lead to him being charged? It was all his own fault. If he had not lost his temper and hit Gerard, his name would never have come up. No one would have been inquiring about him, prompting others to remember the incidents, which were now going to be used to prove him guilty of murder.

The only way he could save himself was to name May. That he would never do. He would just hope that the scales of justice would raise his way.

Jessica had enough confidence in William to believe he would not easily betray May, but she doubted whether he could withstand the vigorous questioning he would be subject to. He needed help. With that intent in mind, she spoke to Douglas,

'May is very upset, Douglas. She has always regarded William as a close friend and fears what could happen to him. I can't believe myself that he could be guilty of murder, but the law can make mistake. He is quite an unsophisticated young man. His words could easily be twisted by a clever barrister. He needs help, Douglas. Could you, perhaps, retain a lawyer to plead his case? It would certainly please May.'

'I suppose you're right,' Douglas agreed. 'I've always liked the lad. Good Scottish stock. His uncle Gordon died recently, I believe, so the poor fellow would be on his own. I'll speak to Driver and, if he will vouch for him, I'll see if I can retain Arthur Lancaster. He's considered one of the best.'

'I'm sure May would be most grateful if you did.'

Jessica felt she had done her best. William's life was now in the lap of the gods. But wasn't it always so. Plan as you may, nobody could predict the future.

William's trial began in the first week of October. Justice Raymond Atkin was surprised that the trial had been brought forward so quickly. It was suggested that it was to lessen the grief of the Reid family but he had a feeling powerful people wanted it over as quickly as possible. But he would not be rushed. He would judge the evidence carefully and give his advice without fear or favour. But in the end it would be up to the jury.

The first day of the trial was taken up with selection of that jury. The number of men eligible for duty had been much reduced through enlistment. Then there were those in essential services who could not be spared, even for a trial as sensational as this. What were left, were often less than suitable. There were more women than usual.

Both lawyers chose carefully. They were not sure whether women would be more or less sympathetic to their case. Fredrick McMillan knew that his evidence, though convincing, was purely circumstantial. Arthur Lancaster's problem was that, as William would not help himself by telling where he had been that night, he had no alibi. It would be his job to find holes in the prosecution's evidence, convince the jury of William's good character, and hope that one of the prosecution witnesses would slip up. All he needed to do was create doubt.

Both lawyers used up their eight challenges before a jury was chosen. All in all, the first day crowd had found it rather boring after a while, but hoped for better entertainment the next day when the trial proper would begin.

CHAPTER 26

There was bigger crowd on day two and many were turned away, disappointed. They would have to wait and read all about it in the Telegraph.

The noisy buzz ceased as Justice Atkin entered, took his seat and indicated he was ready to begin.

To the question, "How do you plead?" William's "Not guilty" had a ring of sincerity that Arthur hoped would impress the chosen twelve.

Fredrick McMillan called his first witness, Police Constable Jenkins, the policeman who had been the first to respond to a report of the accident. Fredrick paused before asking his first question. He wanted to establish that he was in no hurry because he knew he had a firm case.

'Constable Jenkins, would you tell the jury what you encountered when you responded to a report of an automobile accident at Redcliffe.'

Jenkins opened his notebook. 'At 6.22 a.m. on 22. 6. 44, in response to a phone call, I arrived to see a small car, which appeared to have run off the road at Redcliffe Point. It had not gone all the way into the sea because it had become wedged against a large rock. I could see there was a body inside but, because the car was so unstable, I called for assistance. We retrieved the body of a young man who was later identified as Gerard Reid.'

'And the young man was dead?'

'Yes. He appeared to have been dead for some time. He was officially declared dead at, 7.13 a.m.'

'Could you describe his injuries?'

'He had a large gash over his right temple.'

'Was there much blood in the car?'

'No. When I looked there was no blood apart from on his face and smears on the steering wheel but the car was so unstable that it went over the cliff just after we retrieved Mr Reid's body.'

'But you definitely saw no blood when you first looked.'

'Yes, Sir. There was no blood on the floor or the seats.'

'No blood!' Fredrick looked pointedly at the jury.

'No, Sir. No blood at all.'

Arthur Lancaster stood. 'Constable Jenkins, you said, when you looked. Was the car not examined closely?'

'No, Sir. The car was in such a precarious position that we retrieved the body first, but as the car was being pulled up, it slipped and rolled into the sea.'

'So we must rely on your evidence as to the condition of the car?'

'No, Sir. There were two ambulance members who helped in the retrieval.'

'I have just two more questions, Constable. Mr Reid's car was a Bantam with a fold up hood, was it not?

'Yes. That is correct.'

'And was the hood damaged in the accident?'

'Yes, it collapsed.'

'Thank you. Now I wonder if you could describe to us just how the body was situated in the car.'

'It was slumped forward.'

'As if it had fallen into the steering wheel?'

'Yes.'

'As if it had fallen into the steering wheel and covered by the car's hood.' Arthur repeated this sentence slowly, looking towards the jury. 'Thank you, Constable.'

The next witness for the prosecution was the doctor who had performed the autopsy.

'Dr Hobson,' McMillan began, 'could you describe the state of the body when you examined it?'

'It was the body of a young, healthy man. There was very little damage apart from a large gash over his right temple and some bruising on his forehead.'

'Could this bump on the head have caused his death?'

'I thought, at first glance it had but, on examination, discovered that it was not the case.'

'So, Gerard Reid did not die as a result of this blow.'

'No.'

There was a murmur in the courtroom and everyone moved a little closer in their seats.

'You are sure of this?'

'Yes.'

'Then what was the cause of Gerard Reid's death?'

'He died from suffocation.'

The court erupted and Justice Atkin had to call for order.

William, who had been standing quietly, listening to the evidence, shook his head and mouthed a silent, 'no.' His clear, blue eyes clouded with doubt. This was not right.

'Then, Dr Hobson, would you say that Gerard Reid was already dead when the car left the road?' Again, Fredrick turned to the jury as he asked this question.

'I would say so. Yes.'

Arthur was on his feet. He had puzzled over this piece of evidence but felt he had come up with a possible solution, hardly plausible, but enough to put some doubt in the jury's mind.

'Doctor Hobson, I would like to put a proposition to you. Would it be possible, only possible, I mean, that Mr Reid could have sustained his head wound somewhere else, perhaps be disoriented for a time, then driven towards Redcliffe where the effects of the blow to his head affected him to such an extent that he drove off the road and collapsed into the wheel. The hood fell over him and, because he was unconscious, he suffocated. Could this be a possibility?'

Hobson paused. The suggestion was ridiculous, yet stranger things had happened.

'Yes. That could be a possibility, a remote one, but it could be possible.'

'Thank you, Dr Hobson.'

There was a murmur in the gallery as people commented on this answer.

McMillan was immediately on his feet. 'Dr Hobson, what would be the chances of Mr Reid being suffocated in such a manner?'

'One in a million, I would say.'

Laughter greeted this remark. Fredrick was pleased that he had squashed this ridiculous idea but Arthur Lancaster was happy too. Far-fetched the idea might be, but he had created a doubt.

The first witness to be called next day was the taxi driver, Bill Johnstone, who had driven William to Brunswick Street that night. Fredrick had full confidence in this witness. After establishing his name and occupation he began, 'Mr Johnstone, could you tell the jury about a fare you drove to Brunswick Street on the night of 21st. July?'

'At 9.30 that night I was called to Grange Road. My passenger, Mr Forbes, was waiting for me on the footpath. He seemed to be in a hurry. He asked to be taken to Brunswick street.'

'Any particular address in Brunswick Street?'

'No. He said he would tell me when to stop.'

'Go on.'

'He seemed to be rather distracted, upset, you know. So I took special notice of him in my rear vision mirror. He didn't seem dangerous, but you never know. When we were passing Judge Reid's residence he suddenly became agitated, demanded that I stop and was out of the car before it was properly stopped.'

'In his agitated state, did he remember to pay his fare?'

'Yes. He thrust a ten shilling note into my hand before I had even checked the fare.'

'Ten shillings? That seems a bit steep.'

'It was. It was way over the accepted fare. Before I could say anything he was gone. I would have giving him his change but he was gone, you know, I couldn't do anything about it. That's probably why I remembered him, you see.'

'And when you read about the suspicious death of Gerard Reid?'

'I thought I should report it. I didn't know if it was important, you know, but I thought I'd better do it just in case.'

'Later on you were called to Roma Street to view some photos.'

'Yes.'

'And?'

'I was shown several photos and I had no trouble picking him out.'

'You identified William as the young man who went into Gerard Reid's home on the 21st?'

'Yes. It was the same person.'

Arthur stood. 'I have just one question. Did you see Mr Forbes enter Judge Reid's premises?'

'No. It was too dark. It had been raining most of the day and still very misty outside.'

'Thank you, Mr Johnstone.'

A small victory, Arthur thought.

Fredrick was not so confident about the first witness he called the next morning but if he questioned him carefully he could help paint the picture he was trying to create in the jury's mind. Joe Weller had informed him that he did not want to be a witness. He only went to the police station because his wife had nagged him into doing it. He would answer questions asked but had no opinion on the matter at all.

'Mr Weller, your milk run goes along Grange Road, is that correct?'

'Yes.'

'And, on the morning of 22st. July, at 6a.m., did you encounter Mr Forbes?'

'I couldn't say the exact time, but that's right.'

'And what was Mr Forbes doing?'

'He was going into his house.'

'You remarked that he was up early.'

'Yes.'

'And what was his answer?'

'He said he had some early morning business.'

'Some early morning business,' Fredrick repeated. 'And could you tell the members of the jury how Mr Forbes was dressed?'

'He was dressed in a suit.'

'Could you comment on his general appearance?'

'He looked knackered.'

'He looked knackered.' Fredrick looked towards the jury box. 'As if he had run a long way, perhaps?'

'I wouldn't know.'

Fredrick knew he would get nothing more from this witness. 'Thank you, Mr Weller.'

Arthur sensed that Joe was an unwilling witness. Perhaps he could make something of that.

'Mr Weller, have you been a milkman for some time?'

'Thirty odd years.'

'So it would be fair to say that you know most of your customers. Know them by name.'

'Yes. I get to know 'em pretty well, mainly from their orders, but I know most of 'em by name too.'

'So you knew Mr Forbes?'

'Yes. He's been there for a while. I've got to know him and we sometimes have a few words to say.'

'And what kind of person would you say Mr Forbes was?'

'Well, he's a friendly chap and people who've done business with him say he's very helpful.'

'So you would say he is popular among his neighbours?'

'I wouldn't say I know him that well, but the other customers think he's O.K.'

'So, when you saw him that morning, dressed in a suit, what did you think?'

Joe laughed. 'I thought he might have had a night on the town.'

Arthur felt he would not get anything more positive, so thanked and dismissed him.

Fredrick McMillan was very confident about the next witness he was about to call. He had been saving him up for some time. Usually police witnesses were called early in a case, but he had kept the investigating detective for last. He had already planned a dramatic finishing line. He wanted it to be the last words the jury would remember when they retired for the day. It might even make headlines in the Tribune.

Detective Inspector Bright was called and some time was spent explaining how the prisoner had become a suspect. Fredrick paused long enough to impress on the jury that the next questions were of the utmost importance.

'Inspector, when you began interviewing this young man, William Forbes, what was his general demeanour?'

'He seemed quite relaxed and appeared ready to answer questions.

'Did he admit to the fight he had with Gerard Reid?'

'Yes.'

'Did he deny saying, "If you ever say anything about that

woman again, I will kill you"?

'No. He admitted it quite freely.'

'And, when you asked him who was the woman in question, did he tell you?'

'No. He said he'd rather not say.'

Fredrick raised his eyes to show his contempt for the answer.

'Detective, did he admit to taking a taxi to Brunswick Street on the evening of 21st. July?'

'Yes. He said he was the man.'

'When you asked him where, in Brunswick St., he was going, what did he say.'

'He said, "I'd rather not say."

'He'd rather not say.' Fredrick was working up to his grand climax. 'Inspector, did he agree that he was the man in Grange Rd. in the early hours of 22nd?'

'Yes he did.'

'Did you ask him where he had been?'

'He declined to answer.'

'He declined to answer. And what were his exact words?'

Bright began to answer, 'He said ...'

'Let me guess. "I'd rather not say ... I'd rather not say."

Fredrick turned to the jury. "He'd rather not say". 'Ladies and gentlemen, this man is being tried for taking another man's life, but when asked a simple question, to provide a simple answer as to his whereabouts, he says, "I'd rather not say." What game is he playing? .. "He'd rather not say." McMillan shook his head in disbelief.

'Does he take us for fools? Any man, with the threat of execution hanging over him, if he had even a smidgen of evidence that would prove his innocence, would shout it from the rooftops, but this man, this guilty man, who cannot give an answer that will not incriminate him, hides behind a subterfuge of gallantry. He has not been brave enough to offer his life to the service of his country, but he would have us believe that he is here today, bravely facing a charge of murder, because he is protecting the good name of some woman.

'What a joke, what an insult to your intelligence. I say that he cannot tell her name because she does not exist. He is hiding behind some fictitious "damsel in distress" hoping that you will be impressed by his gallantry. Who does he think he is? Sir Galahad?'

He sat down amid laughter from the audience. William was now a figure of fun.

Bright was the last witness called that day. William was taken back to the holding cells and the courtroom cleared. Arthur Lancaster was the last person to leave. He had sat for some time going over the notes he had taken during the day. He was not very confident about his client's chances. If only the boy would speak. Albert did not think he was guilty of Reid's murder, but he was guilty of something. Otherwise why wouldn't he say where he had really been? Did he really believe that justice could be served without a little assistance?

CHAPTER 27

Arthur Lancaster had toyed with the idea of calling William as his first witness the next day, hoping that his appearance of honesty would sway the jurors, but McMillan had reduced him to a figure of ridicule. Now, unless William broke his silence, McMillan would make mincemeat of him. Arthur couldn't take the risk? He spent the evening going over the trial details. Unless he could persuade William to break his silence it would be a disaster. He had a restless night and was not looking forward to the next day when he would begin his defence.

May had been much relieved when Douglas had informed her that he had enlisted the services of Arthur Lancaster to defend her friend.

'He's considered the best defence lawyer in Brisbane. If anyone can get the boy off it will be Lancaster. Not that I necessarily think he is guilty, but the law's a tricky business. Best give him every chance.'

May thanked him profusely. She had been suffering great anxiety ever since she had heard the news. She did not want Willie to suffer but she was terrified for herself if he confessed.

Since then Jessica and Douglas had conspired to keep her ignorant of the snippets of news that filtered out between the time of William's arrest and the actual trial. Great world events such as the steady advance of the Americans from island to island in the Pacific and the failed assassination attempt on Hitler's life filled the headlines and the nightly news. Local news was usually found on the second or third page.

May made their conspiracy easy. She seemed to have lost interest in events around her. Douglas wondered if this change could be another symptom of pregnancy. He remembered the difficult person she had become last time. This was easier to live with. But whatever her moods he would forgive her if she could give him a son.

Each time he came back from a trip up country he waited eagerly for confirmation of his suspicions, even dropping hints, but no announcement was made. It was as if she had no interest in the world around her, as if she had no interest in William's fate.

It was not until day four of the trial May even knew that the trial had begun and it was a headline, inspired by McMillan's final words, that caught her eye.

IS THIS SIR GALAHAD?

Underneath was a sketch of William. May nearly collapsed when she saw it. She realised that her mother and husband had been keeping her in the dark.

I'm not a child, she thought. I am an adult and responsible for Gerard's death. I can't let William be punished for what I have done.

Douglas was away in Toowoomba at the time. May said

nothing about the headline to her mother but later in the morning announced, 'I simply must go into town and look at the new fashions. I've hardly used any of my coupons so I might be able to buy a decent dress for summer. I might even ring Evelyn and suggest we have lunch at Lennons.'

Jessica was pleased that May sounded like her old self. She had also been worried about May's withdrawal. She had held fewer events at *Inverrigan*, she got no pleasure from playing with Flora, she hardly made contact with her girlfriends, she had even lost interest in fashion and was beginning to favour loose, shapeless dresses called "house-coats".

'They are more comfortable Mother. It is not as if I am going anywhere.'

'A day in town sounds lovely, dear. Don't worry about Flora, we will find plenty to do, but you could buy a little treat for her. She does love surprises.'

May had never been in a courtroom before but followed the crowd as they pushed their way into the building. Those who had been following the case knew that it was nearing its close, and the Telegraph's headline had tweaked the interest of others. Most were interested in getting as close to the front as possible. May was happier in the back row.

It was fashionable at the time to wear hat veils so she hoped no one would recognize her. She preferred to be invisible. She could only see the side and back of William's head. She wished she could see his face but, at least, he could not see her. He would have no idea that she was in the courtroom.

She had not reasoned through why she was there, or what

she intended to do. She only knew that she must be there. She would watch proceedings and see what happened.

Arthur Lancaster was fatalistic as he stood to begin his defence. He intended calling two witnesses who would present William as someone of good character, prove that he was no coward then point out the circumstantial nature of the prosecution's case. It was the best he could do, seeing that William refused to help himself.

His first witness was David Driver. He told the court how William had come to him as a young apprentice, had proved reliable and diligent, how he had shown great promise and was now a respected member of his organisation.

'So, you were surprised when Mr Forbes was charged with this crime?' Arthur asked.

'Very surprised. It was totally out of character and I find it impossible to believe he would do such a thing.'

Arthur's next witness gave a similar positive report.

Fredrick McMillan's cross-examination was, at best cursory. He had already planned to remind the jury that good men often do bad things. A good character was no defence against a charge of murder.

Lancaster knew that McMillan's constant references to William's civilian status were damaging, so his next witness was the medical officer who had declared William medically unfit.

McMillan had played on William's civilian status to suggest to the jury that he was a coward. He did not think that the evidence given by the doctor had unduly damaged this tactic

In cross-examination, Fredrick asked, 'When did William Forbes volunteer for service?'

'He was one of the first to volunteer after the fall of France.'

'Medical requirements were quite strict at that time, would you say?'

'Yes. We only passed the fittest.'

'Later in the war, particularly after the Japanese entered, were these requirements modified?'

'That is correct.'

'So, if William Forbes had applied then, would he have been accepted?'

'No. William Forbes did reapply but was again rejected. It seems he had had pneumonia as a child, which left him with weak lungs. He was originally declared unfit for service in the deserts of Africa. He would have been even more unfit in the jungles of New Guinea.'

This was not the reply Fredrick had hoped for but he did not think it would damage his case. He had only played the coward card to give his Sir Galahad remark more power.

Arthur thought the doctor's evidence was a small victory, but would it be enough?

Justice Atkin felt this a suitable time to break for lunch. The buzz of the crowd, discussing the pros and cons of the morning's session, hardly penetrated May's thoughts as she wrestled with her conscience. She knew, from the news item she had read, that Willie had not mentioned her name, even to save himself.

From the evidence she had heard and atmosphere in the room, she felt he would be found guilty. She could not let that happen.

But, if she confessed she would, herself, face a charge of murder. Even if she were to be believed, she would still be found guilty of manslaughter and sent to prison and Willie would also be given a prison sentence because he had tried to dispose of the body. She must find a way to save them both.

During the break she spoke with Arthur Lancaster who agreed that William's chances were not good.

'Then Mr Lancaster, you must call me as a witness. I know where Willie was that night and I know he did not kill Gerard Reid.'

'Mrs Henderson, why haven't you come forward before this? It was your husband who enlisted me.'

'My evidence will embarrass myself and others. I had hoped not to use it. But I cannot see Willie condemned for a crime he did not commit.'

'And you are sure this evidence will prove his innocence?'

'Oh, yes.'

'Then I must contact Judge Atkin immediately. It is very unusual to present a new witness at this late stage. I will have to get his permission.'

Arthur hurried off to speak to the judge. May went back into the courtroom and sat quietly, planning how she could save herself and Willie.

CHAPTER 28

As soon as the court resumed Arthur Lancaster stood, and after a nod from Justice Atkin, said 'I call the next witness, May Henderson'.

May rose and walked slowly to the witness box. She stood there, lost in a world of her own, as the buzz, created by Lancaster's announcement, subsided into a stunned silence.

Why on earth am here? No one has, for one moment, connected me to the crime.

Yet here she was, about to ruin her life. Why was she doing it?

Because she couldn't allow Willie to sacrifice his life for hers. There was a chance, a slim one, that the jury would find him innocent, but it was just that, a slim chance. She couldn't take that gamble. She would not risk Willie's life. She had used his love for her selfishly, for her own ends. Her love had been immature, self-serving, but his was real. And with that thought came a new realisation. She knew now that, not only did he love her enough to die for her, but that she truly, really did love him too.

She took the oath, swearing to tell the truth, the whole truth, and nothing but the truth, sent up a silent prayer to be forgiven for the lie she was about to tell, took a deep breath and waited for the first question from Arthur Lancaster.

'Mrs Henderson, would you please tell the jury what you have told me.'

She looked at William who sat shaking his head and mouthing the words, 'no, no' She stood a little taller. She had wondered whether, at the last moment, her voice would fail her and was quietly surprised to hear it, audible and firm.

'I know William Forbes could not have killed Gerard Reid because he spent that night with me.'

The courtroom erupted in astonishment and Judge Atkin had to call, 'Order' several times before the sound subsided.

'Are you telling the jury that you are the woman whose name was used in the argument?'

'Yes.' May was feeling more confident now. She would get through this. She saw William's look of astonishment. She smiled at him as if to say, 'trust me.'

'And were you the reason why Mr Forbes was in Brunswick Street on the 21st. July?'

'Yes.' She could feel her confidence growing. "I asked him to call, but to get out of the taxi before he got to *Inverrigan*. It was just coincidence that he alighted in front of the Reid residence.'

'And for how long did Mr Forbes remain in your house?'

'He remained all night.'

Another gasp swept through the courtroom and once again Judge Atkin had to call for order.

'So, if he was with you all night, he could not possibly have been anywhere near Redcliffe during the evening or in the early hours of the 22nd?'

'No. He left *Inverrigan* at 5 a.m.'

'Thank you, Mrs Henderson.'

Arthur looked towards the jury and shrugged, as if to say, 'There you are.'

Fredrick was on his feet immediately. He had thought he had a shut and dried case. He was taken aback by May's evidence, but he recovered quickly.

'Mrs Henderson, you say that Mr Forbes spent the night at *Inverrigan*. Can anyone else in the house confirm this?'

'No. We were not in the house. We were in the summerhouse.'

Several titters greeted this announcement.

'Ah, yes. The summerhouse.' Fredrick paused, to give the word full effect. He could see the some of the jurors were leaning forward in their seats. 'The summerhouse. And pray, what were you and Mr Forbes doing in the summerhouse?'

Lancaster was instantly on his feet objecting, but McMillan let it go. He had made his point. He took his time over the next question.

'Mrs Henderson, what you are doing might seem like a noble gesture, but I suggest to you that it is a last ditch stand to save your paramour.' He took a deep breath then thundered, 'Mrs Henderson, are you lying to save your lover from the gallows?'

Until this moment May still felt protected from reality but the word 'gallows' burst that protection.

She had a vision of herself standing on a wooden platform. There was no noose hanging in front of her but the trap door at her feet had just been sprung. As she fell she knew that when she landed it would be into a strange, new world – the real world. All her life, it seemed, she had lived in a fairy tale, with her the heroine in every story. But this was real. She was

Dorothy, expelled from the technicolour world of OZ to the black and white world of Kansas.

No longer would she be May Henderson, the beloved wife of a powerful man. No longer would the world revolve around her, catering to her every whim or fancy. Now she would have to face reality, all the hardship and troubles, all the trials and disappointments of real living. She would even have to face Douglas' wrath. But she knew she could do it. She looked away from her accuser towards the judge.

'Your Honour, when I came into this courtroom, I was a well-known and respected member of this community. I have entertained the greatest in this city. I was the envy of many. When I leave I will be a pariah, a subject of gossip, a disgraced wife, a figure of ridicule. Do you think I would do that just to save a lover?'

Fredrick could feel the power her words were having on the jury. He had to combat that.

'Mrs Henderson, are you trying to suggest that this man is willing to risk death, by hanging, just to protect your name? Mrs Henderson, would you tell the jury why any man would do that?'

May turned her eyes on William and looked at him with a new understanding.

'Because he is an honourable man.'

The jury, and the people in the courtroom who had been holding their breath during this exchange, let out a collective sigh.

Fredrick McMillan knew that May had won, but he gathered himself for one last try.

'Mrs Henderson are you suggesting . . .' but Judge Atkin had heard enough.

'Thank you, Mrs Henderson, you are excused.'

May stepped down and walked serenely towards the door. There was complete silence as people watched this person, whom most had known only through the pages of social magazines, exit the courtroom.

As soon as the doors closed behind her the spell was broken. They found their voices, people stood, turned to their neighbour, wondered whether they should rush out after her, but Justice Atkin pounded his gavel over and over demanding silence. The doors were closed, the sound subsided and most regained their seats.

The drama was not over yet.

Atkin waited until he had complete silence. It gave him time to consolidate his thoughts. This had been a strange trial from the beginning, but no one, in their wildest dreams, had contemplated a climax like this. It would be a talking point among the legal fraternity for some time. He must ensure that his deliberation would honour the occasion.

'Today,' he began, 'we have all witnessed a most unusual happening; a young man willing to risk his life to protect the reputation of another, and a young woman who has destroyed that reputation to save his life.

'For ruined that reputation will be. I sense the frustration most of you are feeling at not being able to race out and spread the news. You will be the centre of every social gathering or back yard chat, for you were here and heard it first. You reporters are already planning the wording of your brilliant headline, your first-hand account of today's events.

'Oh yes, you will all find gold in today's extraordinary

proceedings. But will you also remember the bravery of these two young people? Or will you just remember their transgression of public morals? Will the words adultery and fornication sound louder than nobility and self-sacrifice? Unfortunately I think so.

'As to the trial itself, it has been a travesty of justice. On the flimsiest of evidence, an argument, a taxi ride and an early morning arrival home, a young man's life has been ruined. All three events have now been satisfactorily explained, thanks to the courage of one young woman. I find it hard to understand why this trial was called at all. Circumstantial evidence is always a very shaky foundation on which to build a case and, in this case, it has collapsed.

'I declare this a mistrial. It should never have been called. I demand all record of it to be destroyed and Mr William Forbes to be immediately dismissed without a blemish to his name.

Pandemonium broke out. People who wished to express their opinion of the judge's speech had to shout to be heard above the arguments that had broken out and reporters jostled with spectators in a race to be out first.

The one point of silence was the dock, where William sat quietly, trying to take in all that had occurred. His mind had not yet fully processed the fact that he was free. He was still grappling with May's evidence. She had lied, under oath. He could understand the reason, but, if she could lie about that, could she have also lied about how Gerard died?

Arthur pushed his way through the melee. 'You are free to go William?'

'Oh, yes. Thank you. What do I do? Can I just walk out?'

'There will be a few formalities, but then you will be free, though I fear that there will be a feeding frenzy with the press. I will try to arrange transport for you as quickly as possible.'

'But May? Do you know where she is?'

'I'm not sure but I expect she has already left. Perhaps, as soon as you are alone, you should ring and find out.'

'Thank you.'

As William was escorted from the courtroom, Arthur Lancaster contemplated his next move, for it had been Douglas, May's husband, who had retained him. Would the man still be willing to foot the bill?

CHAPTER 29

May was still coming to terms with the new world she was about to enter as she left the courtroom. A veil seemed to be protecting her from reality but she knew that it would soon be pulled away. At the back of her mind she knew she would have to open it and walk through, but she needed a small interlude before she began the new life that awaited her there.

It was fortunate there was a taxi waiting at the rank. She hailed it, gave her address and during the ride home began to make some sense of what was ahead of her. She felt reborn, a new person with a new, uncharted life. Every feature of her former world was gone. At twenty-four she would have to learn how to be part this new, strange universe.

A cloud of weariness engulfed her. She needed rest. She could and would get through this. She would have a future, but first she must sleep.

Jessica and Flora were on the side veranda when the taxi pulled up. Flora, with her grandmother's encouragement, had been busy, drawing pictures.

'Mummy is home, Flora. Come and show her your lovely drawings.' She had believed that May had spent the morning shopping and was surprised to see she was not carrying any parcels. 'Did you have a good day May? Did you catch up with Evelyn?'

'I will tell you later.' May walked past her into the house.

'Mummy, look at my picture.'

'Not now, Flora. Mummy needs to lie down.'

Jessica saw the excitement in the child's eyes dulled to disappointment. She hugged her precious granddaughter to her as she watched her daughter walk through the hall and up the stairs. Something was wrong. May would need her, but she could wait. First, she must cheer up Flora, then find something to occupy her little mind so that she would not feel neglected.

'Mummy is tired, darling, after a big day in town. She needs a little sleep, just like you do after you have been to the park. I think we should go and see what Beppi is doing in the vegetable garden. He might take you to see if the hens have laid any eggs.'

May was not sleeping. She lay on her bed, eyes closed, trying to grow into the person she now was. She was no longer May Swann or Mrs May Henderson, with all the prestige that that persona had given her. Now she was the adulteress, the scarlet woman, to be shunned by all decent members of society. That was if she survived at all.

She had not only shamed herself. She had brought shame on Douglas and the Henderson name. Would he kill her? She thought not. Her notoriety would save her that. But would he harm her? Oh yes, he would find a way. But how?

Was she sorry for what she had done? No. She was desperately sorry that it had had to be done, but she was not sorry that she had done it. She could not have let Willie die or spend his life in prison for a crime he did not commit, even to save herself.

She was surprised to discover that she was not afraid. In fact she was looking forward to the future. For the first time in her life she now knew what love really meant. It wasn't all that romantic claptrap she had read about in books. It wasn't the sexual activities that were called love. It was knowing, with every fibre in your body, that this was the one person in your life who mattered more than life itself. She loved Willie and, no matter what the future held, she would always love him. She would love him till the day she died.

The thought of Willie brought her mind back to the here and now. What had happened after she had left the courthouse? Surely her evidence had proved his innocence. What if he had been found guilty even after her evidence?

As soon as Flora was happy, chatting to Beppi, Jessica hurried upstairs to confront her daughter. May, eyes still closed, was lying on top of her bed but stirred when she heard her mother enter.

'May,' Jessica whispered, 'are you well? Is there anything I can do for you?'

'No Mother, there is nothing anyone can do. I'm afraid I have very bad news for you. I didn't go shopping. I went to court to listen to Willie's trial. I could see that it was going badly so I told the court he hadn't done it.'

Jessica almost collapsed with shock. 'Oh, May, what have you done? Did you tell them everything that happened?'

'No. I told them that Willie had been with me all night so he couldn't have killed Gerard.'

'Oh, my God, May. Do you know what you have done?'

'Yes, Mother. I do. I have made myself a pariah. None of my friends will want to know me but I have saved Willie's life.'

'But Douglas. He will kill you.'

'No, I don't think he will. But he will throw us out of the house. I'm sorry for you and Flora but I couldn't let Willie hang.'

The fortress of protection that Jessica had built around her life crumbled. All the neglect, the insults, the humiliations she had borne were for nothing. May had destroyed, not just her own future, but that of her daughter. What would happen to Flora?

'May we must leave here, at once, before Douglas gets back.'

'No.' May sat up. Suddenly she was the one taking charge. She had created this mess. She would see it through. She was not going to run away like some frightened child. She would face her future, whatever it was to be. She would be strong for her daughter, her mother, and most of all for Willie, for Douglas would surely take his vengeance out on him too.

'No, Mother. I am going to stay here till he returns. He has always been good to me so I will give him the satisfaction of throwing me out. I don't know what we will do after that. We will probably have to leave Brisbane and I will have to go to work, though what I will be good for I do not know.'

'What about William? Is he free?'

'I do not know. I left as soon as I had given my evidence. But surely they couldn't convict him after what I said?'

'May, I have always advised you, but this time I do not know what to say.'

'You do not have to say anything, Mother. I am a grown woman and more than capable of thinking for myself. I made this decision knowing full well what the consequences would be. I am sorry that you and Flora will have to suffer too, but that is better than having a good man die.'

She stood and walked towards her wardrobe. 'We had better begin packing. I am sure Douglas will hurry home when he gets the news. Poor Douglas, he was a bit of an autocrat but he didn't deserve this.'

Jessica looked anew at her daughter. This was not the child she had known, always looking to her for advice. This was a grown woman, willing to take responsibility for her actions, ready to face the world without protection from anyone. But would she be able to sustain it? When cruel reality struck and life got hard, how could she, who had never known anything but security, survive?

The telephone rang and they both hurried down the stairs to answer it. May reached it first.

'Willie,' she shouted.

'It's Willie,' she informed Jessica.

'Oh Willie darling, are you free?'

'He's free. The judge declared a mistrial. He's free.'

Jessica nodded then walked away to let them speak in private. She had a crisis to face, but this time she was in unknown territory. This time, it seemed, her future was in the hands of others.

'No, Willie. Douglas is not home yet.'

'No. I will wait till he gets here. I don't want to run away like a fugitive. I will face his anger then walk away. He won't kill me, I know, and he can't destroy my reputation. I have already done that myself. I am afraid I have done that to yours too. I am sorry but it is done. We have only the future to look forward to.'

'Of course I want to spend it with you. That is, if you will still have me?'

'No, do not come here. That would enrage him and he might do anything. Please, wait till it is over. I will come to you. I will ring and you could meet me in the city. I love you, Willie. I know that now. I really, really do.'

Douglas had fumed, at first, that he was away from Brisbane when the scandal broke, but now he was glad. It had given him the time and space to absorb the shock, and plan what he would do. She must be punished but he must retain his dignity.

If she had already fled he would hunt her down. If she were still in Brisbane he would see that her disgrace was complete. She would never be able to show her face in decent society. As for William, he would never get work in the state again.

He had feared there might be a member of the press at the station when he arrived but was able to slip into Brisbane unobserved, because the Rome Street Station was crowded with troops from down south, being transferred from the Kyogle Street interstate station, to the narrow gauge line, for their journey north.

He was fortunate to get a taxi almost immediately but had not formulated a plan before he arrived at *Inverrigan.* Listening to the crunch of his feet on the gravelled path as he walked towards the front door helped calm his mind.

Jessica had been keeping watch from an upstairs window so his arrival was not unexpected. She was fearful of the confrontation, but stood with her daughter and granddaughter at the foot of the stairs. She had weathered many storms in her life and survived. She would survive this too.

Douglas surveyed the tableau that greeted him, May at floor

level, holding Flora's hand, Jessica on the bottom step and four cases to the side of them. The adults stared at each other, no one willing to make the first move, but Flora had no such restriction.

'Daddy,' she cried and flew into his open arms. 'Daddy, we're going on a holiday.'

Douglas dragged his gaze from the wife who had betrayed him and gave his full attention to his little daughter.

'Are you now, pet. Are you going to go away just when your Daddy has come home to see you?' He pulled a sad face.

Flora considered this thought then laughed. 'You can come too.'

'I think not, darling.'

Still holding his daughter on his arm, he walked towards his wife.

'You are leaving, I see. Good. But not with my daughter. You can go to hell for all I care but Flora is mine. She stays with me.'

May looked at her daughter snuggling into her father, arms around his neck. She would not have admitted it, but secretly she was relieved. One of her fears had been the kind of a life Flora would have to lead when they left. She was willing to give up the comforts of her own former life but should she inflict the same punishment on her daughter. Now she knew that her daughter would be safe. Douglas loved her and would always see to her future wellbeing.

She did not move towards them, just gave her daughter a sad smile. She would make this parting as unemotional as possible so that Flora would find it easier to forget her.

'Very well Douglas. I think she will have a better life with you.' Then to her daughter, 'Goodbye Darling. Be good for your father.'

She took a suitcase in each hand and walked slowly towards the front door. Jessica looked from the face of her darling granddaughter to the receding back of her daughter then reached down to pick up her suitcase.

'Are you leaving us too, Jess?' Douglas said. 'She has to go, but you, you have a choice. Leave with her and you will never see Flora again, for I swear I will take her to another country rather than let you near her. It's your choice, Jess, May or Flora.'

Jessica looked from mother to daughter. Her heart was being torn in two.

Flora, as if understanding the drama being enacted in front of her, leant forward, waved her fingers and called, 'Jess, Jess.'

The decision was made. Jessica knew that Douglas meant what he said. She also knew that her surrender would make her even more subservient to him, but she could not walk away from the child. May was an adult and would have William. She could not bear a life without her darling Flora.

Douglas had defeated her once again. She had no illusions about her future. She would be at his beck and call for the rest of her life but she would accept this life of servitude. She would never see May again but at least she would have the satisfaction of watching Flora grow. 'I will stay.' she said and put down her case

As a child, Flora would sometimes have a vision of the back of a woman wearing a tan coat, a small hat and carrying a suitcase in each hand. When she asked Jess who the woman was Jessica said 'I have no idea darling. Perhaps it was just a picture you have seen in a book.'

CHAPTER 30

May caught the tram into town and rang William from the post office. She was surprised at how calm she felt. She knew he would come and she knew they could make a future together.

He arrived, relieved that she was unharmed. He took her in his arms and kissed her, uncaring of passers-by. 'May, I still can't believe that you have come to me. Do you really want to spend the rest of your life with me?'

'Yes, Willie. I want to live my life with you.'

'And so you shall, but my rooms are very small. Would you like me to book a room for you in an hotel?'

'No Willie. I don't mind if we have to live in a tent as long as we are together.'

They caught a tram back to Grange Road and William, shamefacedly introduced her to his two rooms above the shop. 'It's been enough for me. I'm sorry it is not larger.'

May looked around. It was small, smaller than she had imagined, but tidy, but she could live there. 'It has all we need, a living room and a bedroom. Do you eat out?'

'No. This is my kitchen.' He opened, what she had thought to be a cupboard. Inside was a two-burner, hot plate. 'I can boil and fry and I make toast with this' and he held up a wire and mesh contraption which could sit on top of the gas flame.

May burst into tears.

'May, I'm sorry there is so little. I will do better.'

'Oh you darling, silly boy, I am not crying over this. I'm crying because I am so useless. I do not know how to cook. I do not know anything about the preparation of food, just how to eat it. I am going to be of no use to you at all.'

'Darling, I don't love you because you will be of use to me. I love you because you are you. I am used to cooking for myself. Just to have you here, looking at me while I do it, will be heaven.'

The first meal he cooked for her was bacon and eggs and May declared that it was the best meal she had ever eaten.

They sat together in the one, soft chair, fondling gently and speaking optimistically about the future. On this, the first night of their future together, they were as shy as young lovers on their first date. Eventually weariness overcame them. William led his beloved girl to his single bed and May experienced, for the first time, lovemaking that was wholly without design, just the giving of two people to each other in love.

Afterwards, curled up in each other's arms, they spoke about the trial.

'May, I cannot thank you enough for what you did, but were you not frightened to lie under oath?'

'It had to be done, Willie. If I had told the truth we would both now be in prison. But I am through with telling lies and half-truths. From now on I will only speak the truth. I have other things to confess too, and I must tell them now, if we are to have any future together.'

William thought she was going to explain about the verdict of suffocation. It had been worrying him ever since he had heard it. He was not sure he wanted to hear what had really happened. The accidental fall he could understand. It was not her fault. But it was what happened next that he didn't want to think about. He could imagine the fear she had felt when she thought he was dead but then to discover that he was still breathing. Was it possible that May, his beautiful May, could then have made her fear a reality?

He steeled himself. She needed to confess. He had to listen.

'Willie, what I tell you will shock you but it must be said. You know Douglas' main reason for marrying me was to beget a son, but I soon realized that he was sterile.'

This was not the conversation he expected. He tried to interrupt but May continued. 'Partly to give him that desire but mainly to protect my own lifestyle, I enticed you into making love to me so that I could conceive.'

William was shocked. 'May, you don't mean . . .'

'Yes. I know you think you had seduced me but it was the other way around. I knew that you would do anything for me so I led you on. As soon as I knew we had succeeded I terminated the affair.'

'But that means . . .'

'Yes. It means that Flora is your daughter, but only through biology. In every other way she is Douglas' daughter. They love each other and are bound together as only a father and daughter can be. We must never break that bond.'

'May, this is very hard to take in.'

'I know, Willie, but believe me we must, for Flora's sake. There is more.' She closed her eyes and took a deep breath to give her the strength to go on.

'I knew Douglas still wanted a son so, recently, I rekindled our romance.' She saw the look of horror in his eyes. She touched his face.

'Forgive me, Willie, but I used you again, and that is what brought about all this disaster. When I think of how many lives have been affected because of my selfishness I am so ashamed. I am sorry that Gerard died. I'm sorry that you had to go through all that nastiness. But something wonderful has come out of it. It made me realise what love really was. I love you, Willie, and want to spend the rest of my life with you.'

William held her close. He could still hardly comprehend what she was saying but he knew it changed nothing. He felt his heart would burst from happiness. He knew he could forgive her anything. She loved him. That was enough. Nothing else mattered. His life was complete.

'Willie, there is more. There is another result, which I hope will please you as much as it pleases me. I am pregnant again, with your child, and if you can forgive me, we three can have a happy life together.'

William was overcome with all this information. He had been used. He had a daughter but most of all there was a chance that he and May could make a happy family of their own.

'Oh May,' was all he was capable of saying for some time, but eventually he managed to get his thought together.

'May, there is nothing to forgive. You love me now. That is all that matters and to have proof of our love will be the greatest gift of all.'

May sighed with relief. Though she had known that Willie loved her, she was not sure, till now, that she would be forgiven. She vowed she would spend the rest of her life making sure that he never regretted his decision.

'And is that the end of your confession?' he asked.

'Yes. I confess that all my life I have been selfish and

manipulating but I will try never to be like that again.'

They kissed to seal the pact then May curled her back into William's chest and was soon asleep. William stayed awake longer, wondering why May had not told him everything. Perhaps Arthur Lancaster's strange explanation could have been possible, but he could not believe it. He was sure that Gerard was already dead when he and Jessica had put his body in the car, but perhaps?

No, Gerard had died in the summerhouse, which meant that May had not told the whole story, but he would have to forgive her this one omission, and pretend he believed she had told him the whole truth, if there was to be a future for himself, May and his unborn child.

CHAPTER 31

As May walked through the door, Douglas experienced a strange sensation. It was as if he had moved out of his body and stood to one side, observing a frozen tableau – a sturdy, greying man in his fifties, a small girl in his arms, a slim middle aged woman mid-way between them and an open door.

'Well, Douglas Henderson, how are you going to deal with this situation?' he asked of himself, as he watched that person fighting to control the surges of emotion - anger, surprise, regret, revenge.

Douglas took deep breaths until he felt he was in control of himself again. 'Jess, take Flora with you and go to the kitchen. Tell Rosa I do not want dinner tonight. Then I want you and Flora to remain upstairs till morning as I do not wish to be disturbed.'

He stood, granite hard, showing no emotion, but Jessica knew the effort needed to contain this calm. She took Flora from his arms and hurried off to relay his instructions

When Jessica and Flora were gone he went to his study, locked the door and took down an unopened bottle of Macallan whisky with the intention of getting seriously drunk.

May's calm acceptance of his dismissal had disturbed him. It was not the reaction he had expected. On the train coming back he had gone over one scenario after another; she would have run away, she would have been penitent, she would have been defiant. But the reality had been so different. She had calmly walked out of his life. She had made no demands. She had shown no resistance when he reclaimed Flora nor when Jess had chosen to stay. She had just picked up her cases and was gone.

And her leaving had left a hole, a great gaping hole in his life. It manifested itself as a palpable pain in the pit of his stomach and though he drank glass after glass of the fiery liquid he could not dull it, nor could he gain the oblivion he desired. He should have been paralytic but his ache remained and his mind active, planning ways he would get his revenge.

Towards morning, when he had drunk himself sober again he finally realised that it was not his ego that was hurting but his heart. He had always thought he loved May, but it had been a possessive love. She was his therefore he loved her. This was something different, an emotion he had had no previous knowledge of and it frightened him.

He realised that he loved her for herself and always would. He would never deliberately see her again but he could never harm her, and he knew that nobody would ever take her place.

Douglas had been brought up to think that showing emotion was weak but, when he at last admitted his feelings, he put his head in his hands and cried, not gentle tears, but agonising moans. Hot, salty water splashed from his eyes into his nose, mouth and hands.

But, like every storm, there came a time when the tears ceased and a kind of peace settled on him. He could look on what had happened and accept it. The anger was still there, the desire for revenge and the feeling of regret, but he could live with it. He still had a life to live and a beautiful daughter to provide for. That was something. He would not allow this scandal to destroy her life. If he showed no reaction people would soon forget. It would be as if May had never existed in their life.

He stood, and at last felt the effects of his drinking. He managed to get to his room without falling and, not bothering to undress, threw himself on his bed. He knew that on waking he would have the mother of all headaches but that too could be endured. He would live and prosper.

Across town May was also coming to terms with her new life. She had been used to the luxury of a double bed and as she slept she gradually occupied most of the mattress and all of the pillow. William was forced up against the wall and spent the rest of the night resting his head on his arm, but he would not have had it any other way.

The first rays of morning, peeping through the wooden shutters, illuminated the face, the hair, of his beloved. This must be how heaven feels, he thought.

He would have liked to have stayed there forever but cramp spreading down his neck to his back threatened to make him a permanent cripple so, trying not to wake his sleeping beauty, he edged himself to the end of the bed and onto the floor.

May stirred, but did not wake. He tiptoed into the living room, dressed, filled a kettle with water from the sink in the skillion and heated it on the gas stove.

The sound of the whistling kettle woke her. It took her a minute or two to remember where she was. She had a wonderful feeling of contentment. She watched through the open door as William measured out the tealeaves and poured in the boiling water. He frowned then looked towards the bedroom.

'What is troubling you, Willie?' she asked.

'Oh. May. You are awake. I just realised that I do not know how you like your tea.'

'White please, a little milk and one teaspoon of sugar.' She sat up, covering her nakedness with a sheet. 'Willie, you are amazing. You know how to make tea.'

'It is nothing. You just pour the hot water onto the leaves.'

'Will you teach me? The next time you can watch me. Then I will be able to make two things, tea and toast. We could live on that.'

'Not for long, I think. But you are such a clever girl, I'm sure you will soon be the best cook in the world.'

'Thank you, Willie, but I am afraid you will have to eat many dreadful failures before that will be true. But I do want to learn. Before, I never thought of food, except to eat it. It will be a tremendous adventure learning how to cook it. The first thing I must buy is a cook book.'

'That too, but I think the very first thing we must buy is a larger bed.'

'Oh Willie, was it so uncomfortable? Did I push you out? Did you get any sleep?'

'I didn't need sleep. It was enough that I could watch you sleeping beside me, but today we must see if we can find a bed big enough, but one that will fit into this small room.'

'I will go to Hick's. They have the best furniture and they know me there.'

May had forgotten, in her new state of happiness that, to the rest of Brisbane, she was a shamed woman, an adulteress. Judge

Atkin's words had been accurate. A salacious account of the outcome of the trial had appeared in all newspapers in Queensland and beyond. It was only pictures of General MacArthur landing at Palo Beach in Leyte that made her old news, but that was still days away. On the morning she went shopping she was still the main topic of gossip in Brisbane.

As she entered the store, May became conscious of the stares and whispers but she ignored them, thinking that she was being oversensitive. It wasn't until she was in the bedding department that it became real.

'I see, Mrs Henderson, that you are in need of a new, double bed.'

The words were spoken by Bernard, the head salesman, well known to May. Formerly he would have been fawning over her but the smirk on his face, the tone of his voice and the stress on the word double, left her in no doubt about her changed status She had been used to being a valued customer, treated with courtesy and accommodation. Now she was someone to be sneered at, to be treated with contempt.

May was broken. She wanted to run away, but she had been part of society for so long, the years of training saved her. The face she presented to Bernard held no sign of shame.

'I beg your pardon; my name is May Swann and I see nothing here suitable to my needs.' She walked slowly through the store, head high, expression non- committal. Let them laugh, she thought. I will never spend a penny in this store again.

Once outside the store her show of courage collapsed. Her legs trembled and she bowed her head, unwilling to meet the eyes of passers-by. She couldn't even find the courage to enter a tram but walked home, the happiness of the morning vanished.

William had left with her, intending to report back to work at Drivers, so she was surprised, but happy to see him when she arrived home.

'Willie, oh Willie,' she cried and threw herself into his arms. Between sobs she told him of the disgrace she had experienced. He comforted and petted her. Gradually her misery diminished.

'At least I now know them for what they are,' she consoled herself as she wiped her eyes. 'They will never get my custom again.'

'That is good to hear,' William replied, a wry smile playing on his lips, 'because I am afraid we would not have been able to afford them anyway. I am sorry, May, but I have lost my job. Mr Driver was very nice about it but told me that, for the good of the company, he would have to dispense with my services. As we have been working on defence contracts he has given me generous severance pay but I am no longer an employee of Driver and Hoe.'

'Oh, Willie. I am so, so sorry. I know how much your work meant to you. I wonder if Douglas made him do it? Or he may have thought he had to do it in solidarity. You must really wish that you had never met me.'

'Never. You are my life. Compared to the sufferings of people around the world this is nothing. Driver's is not the only architectural firm in the world and my work is good enough to stand on its own. For the present, I will find any work I can. I have a small inheritance from my uncle and with the severance pay I will be able to open my own business when all this has been forgotten. As soon as the war is over there will be a great demand for new buildings.'

'Do you think so, Willie? But what will you do in the meantime?'

'I know how to build as well as design so I could hire myself out to any builder who will have me, but even if the blacklist extends to them, there is such a manpower shortage that I will be able to get a job to tide us over.'

With that happy thought they began to plan their future.

CHAPTER 32

William had found the public reaction to him, because of the scandal, different from May's. Yes, he too was an item of gossip but, instead of being a pariah, he was regarded as a hero, not because he had been willing to sacrifice himself for May, but because he had cuckolded an important member of the establishment.

'G'day, Mr Forbes,' Joe Weller waved at him and got down from his milk cart. 'Just wanted to say, wasn't my fault I went to court. The Misses made me. Always knew you was innocent and you proved me right. Told 'em you was only chasing pussy. I was right, eh.' He patted William on the back. 'Good for you mate.' Then he jumped back on his cart.

A letter arrived in the post.

Dear Mr Forbes, it began. *I am writing to say how sorry I am that I gave evidence about you. It was only because of the ten bob that I even remembered you and it was only because you got out in front of Justice Reid's place that I reported you in the first place. But thanks to the lady it all got sorted out in the end. I reckon she's a bit of all right. I'd stick with her if she was mine. Best of luck. I reckon I owe you a free fare any time you're interested.*

Underneath was an almost undecipherable signature but William realised that the letter was from the taxi driver who had driven him to *Inverrigan* on that fateful night.

Some of his former friends went out of their way to congratulate him, but he quickly realised that the slaps on the back and the good wishes were only because they wanted more details about his sex life. They were looking for gossip to share with others over an ale or too. He was horrified at their innuendos and sexual references. He had to restrain himself from becoming involved in physical retaliation. Within days he was also avoiding anyone he had formerly known.

He and May became hermits in their tiny rooms.

'May, we can't stay here where everybody knows us.'

'Do you mean leaving Brisbane?'

'Would you mind that so much, May?'

'I don't know, Willie. I've never lived anywhere else, except when I went to New Zealand. But it would feel like running away.'

'Perhaps we could move to another suburb. Somewhere where nobody knows us.'

'Willie, I will be happy anywhere as long as we are together.'

'And the first thing we will do when we find a place is to buy a bigger bed,' William laughed, but he did not mean it as a joke.

Douglas began to plan his future without May. Ewan Henderson had instilled in his children the need to protect ones public reputation. Douglas was not going to let his marriage disaster become a source of ongoing material for gossipmongers. First he must put the whole scandal behind him. If anybody expected him to show signs of anger, revenge or anguish they would be sadly disappointed. He had never been a man of gossip and had

had long experience in staring down unwanted criticism. He would go on as he always had, attending to his duties, visiting the club and making important decisions. The gossip rags would soon lose interest when some other scandal or murder happened. He would not allow old gossip to damage Flora's future.

Because the war was going so well there had been less need for fundraising or morale boosting so fewer entertainments were being held at *Inverrigan* of late. It would be easy to curtail them altogether. Soon May's exploits would be forgotten, or remembered as just another war story. He had a plan, which had been germinating in his brain for some time. Now he would act on it.

'Jess,' he commanded later in the day, 'I want everything belonging to May in this house to be gone, every picture, every present, anything remotely to do with her to be destroyed. It must be as if she never existed. No one is ever to mention her name again. Most of all, I want Flora to have no memory of her. Children soon forget if not reminded. If she should ask about her mother, tell her she died. Tell her anything but obliterate that woman from her mind. You and I together will be enough for her.'

During his early morning soul searching on the day after May's departure he had decided that he would never marry again, partly to deny May. Unless he divorced her she could not marry William. But he also knew that he would never love another woman enough to take her as a wife. This would mean that Flora would be his only child and, as a girl, she would never inherit. So, if she was to have a future, he must make another fortune for her that was not part of the family inheritance.

The idea had first come from a conversation he had had with Hermas Vandermeer, a Dutch refugee from Java, whose family had lived there for four generations. He had seen his vast interests in the Islands and Europe disappear during the conflicts, but was very optimistic about the future. He and Douglas had several discussions about the possibilities that the post war would offer.

'When this war is over I will not be returning to Java, Douglas. Oh, the Dutch might get back, for a time, but the days of colonisation are numbered, not just for us, but for England and the other European countries which have made their fortunes through exploitation of peoples we considered inferior to ourselves. The natives have seen us brought to our knees by the Japanese, Asian like themselves. They know it is now their time.

'I will not go home to Holland, for it has never been home to me. No. When the war is finished I will gather up what is left of my fortune and migrate to this country. We should join together you and I, Douglas. With my money and your knowledge of the pastoral industry we could make a fortune. We should get into the cattle business. I tell you it will be huge. When the war is over, Douglas, and I am again a wealthy man, I will become your partner. Together we will rebuild the world.'

Among the many American servicemen Douglas had met in the course of his work and at his home, were young men whose families were cattle ranchers. They had spoken about shorthorns and crossbreeds suitable for the vast northern parts of Australia. Why shouldn't he start his own empire? The Hendersons had originally farmed cattle in Scotland. It was in his blood. The war was as good as won. His country didn't need him anymore. There was nothing urgent to keep him here. As soon as it would not appear as a sign of retreat, he would resign his commission, consolidate his personal wealth then take an extended trip to the United States and the British Isles to study breeding and speak with experienced men in the field.

Flora would have her own fortune and this time there would be no clause to preclude female inheritance.

South Brisbane grew from the development of wharves along the Brisbane River. Commercial buildings and hotels sprang up to facilitate business and provide rest and recreation for bullock drivers. By the turn of the century it had become a thriving city, home to waves of unskilled migrants, willing to take any work to gain a foothold in their new country. By the 1940s it had developed a seedy reputation but most of the inhabitants were honest, hard-working people who had little interest in the goings on of those who saw themselves as the important and influential of Queensland.

It was to this suburb that William brought May. There would be little chance of her running into any of her old friends in such a place and work would be easy to find.

In former time there had been a number of large homes in this suburb but as the population increased they had been subdivided into two or three residences. May and William chose one of these. Compared to their rooms in the Grange they were quite spacious. There were three rooms, a large kitchen and the back veranda had been converted into a bathroom and porch. However, sewerage had not reached the area, so the outhouse was a long way from the back steps. May was so happy with the idea of her own house that she didn't mind this small inconvenience.

She wandered from room to room planning her new home. 'This front room will be our drawing room,' she declared, spreading her arms. In her mind she could see leather lounges, elegant side tables and bright Persian rugs. In reality there was cracked linoleum and one old horsehair sofa.

'I was thinking it could become my office when I start my own business,' William suggested but May was already moving on to the next room.

'This will have to be the main bedroom. There will be enough room for a big double bed, a dressing table and a couple of robes.'

'A double bed definitely, but perhaps I could build in the rest of the furniture. It is a new idea called "built ins", does not take up as much room and is easier to keep tidy. I have read about it in a trade book and should have no trouble building it.'

'Oh, Willie, how clever you are. I'm sure it will look lovely.

She moved on 'Now this room. It really should be a dining room, but then where shall we put the nursery?' She was already planning a grand nursery, similar to the one Flora had.

'I think, May that we can dispense with a dining room. The kitchen is quite big enough for a table and chairs, and I don't think we will be entertaining guests for a few years yet.'

'I'm so sorry, Willie. I keep forgetting I am not still at *Inverrigan.*'

William put his arm around her and pulled her to him. 'Do you mind so much, May?'

She snuggled into him and put her head on his chest. 'Of course I don't, silly. I don't miss a thing about my old life, but I forget sometimes. After all, it was all I knew for more than twenty years, but this will be the rest of my life. It's like a grand adventure and I will be sharing it with you, and our baby, when it comes. Do you want a boy or a girl?'

'My beautiful May, I could not care less. All I pray is that it will be as wonderful as you.'

The kitchen was the best of the rooms. It was by far the largest room in the house, louvered windows facing east, cream walls and shiny, almost new linoleum. It also contained a Kooka gas stove and an icebox.

'At least this room is ready to move into. All we need here are table and chairs,' May said.

'And crockery, pots and pans and cutlery,' William reminded her.

'But look, Willie. Look, a Kooka. There are four jets and an oven. I can learn to cook lots of things on this beautiful stove.'

'And so you shall, my darling. We must remember to add a cookery book to our shopping list.'

That night, their last at Grange Road, they disagreed happily about what would be essential and what could be left till later. May was disappointed that a wireless was not on the list but William promised that they would buy one as soon as he got work. He had taken out a mortgage to buy the house and had money in the bank from his small inheritance and his severance pay but, unlike May, he knew that it must be used sparingly. His early life and his uncle's thrifty habits had taught him that money was hard earned but quickly spent unless a close watch was kept. *"Watch the pennies and the pounds will take care of themselves"* had been his uncle's oft repeated motto and William had taken it to heart from an early age.

CHAPTER 33

William found work with the tramways. He was part of a team of maintenance workers. He changed his suit for a pair of overalls and rode a black bike with a basket in front, which contained a can full of oil. He rode all along the tram lines, oiling the points and documenting any wear and tear.

William had not been part of an old boy's network. Though he was friendly and outgoing he had no real friends. It was only through his association with Driver and Hoe that he had become one of the young people who frequented the entertainments at *Inverrigan*. Now he was a member of a gang of maintenance men but spent most of his day alone and spoke to few people.

Like everyone else in the building industry he had been looking forward to the building boom that would follow with the cessation of hostilities. As he rode the streets of Brisbane, he tried not to compare his dreams with the reality he now lived.

It was light years away from the life he had thought would be his, but it was honest toil and he regarded coming home to May at the end of each day as rich compensation.

The next few months were both the happiest and the hardest of May's life. The love she and Willie shared was so real, so complete. There was never a moment's doubt that it would last as long as they lived. But the ordinary things of living, the day-to-day chores, left her feeling inadequate, frustrated and tired.

May was learning the hard realities of life. There was no one there to provide the services she had been used to. She was cleaner, cook and washerwoman.

Tired - She had never been so tired in all her life. Willie left for work at seven thirty in the morning and did not get home till after five, so she was alone all day, doing all the work that had been done by servants at *Inverrigan*. She had never given a thought to how meals were cooked, beds made, rooms cleaned and washing done. Now she knew that every task had to be performed by someone, and she was that someone.

Willie was not demanding and would happily have lived with sausages and semi squalor so long as they were together but May wanted to do everything perfectly.

'May, do not push yourself too hard. Learning domestic skills takes time, just as everything else in life.'

'But you've never worked on the lines before and you're managing.'

'That takes nothing but following orders. I am part of a team. You are trying to be the whole team by yourself. Give it time.'

'I know you're right, Willie, but I want to make everything perfect for you.'

'Everything is perfect, darling. I have you.'

May knew he meant it, but just the sight of him coming home exhausted from a day's labour made her try harder. She wanted her home to be a reflection of the love they had.

The job she hated most was washing. There was no laundry, as such, only a cement slab by the back stairs that contained cement washing tubs, a washboard and wringer and a fireplace containing a copper. This had to be filled from the taps over the tubs, and a fire lighted underneath. If hot water was needed in the tubs it had to be bailed out from the copper. When sheets and clothes had been boiled in the copper they were transported to cold water in the sinks by using a copper stick. Dirty clothes had to be scrubbed on a washboard. Everything had to be rung out by a ringer, put into clean water, then rung out again to get rid of the excess water. Everything was then hung on the long wire line that was stretched between two poles and raised with a prop.

As there was only one copper, washing days had to be negotiated with the family living in the other half of the converted house. They consisted of a husband and wife and four children. May felt they had first priority.

She was always exhausted after washing day so Willie got into the habit of bringing home fish and chips on that day to save her the added stress of cooking a meal.

May quickly became less fussy about dirt, would use towels longer and change her dresses less often. The hardest article to wash was William's overalls. They were made from white calico and showed every bit of dirt and tar that he came in contact with every day. She soon learnt that she could not remove the tar stains but scrubbed and scrubbed until every other stain was gone.

'The boys say I have the whitest overalls in the state,' William told her proudly.

CHAPTER 34

1945

May's neighbours, the Bazzinas, came originally from Malta. They were the first persons of European background with whom May had ever come in close contact. Of course there had been Rosa and Beppi but they were servants. Because of the structure of the house there were several facilities they had to share, not only the laundry, but the front gate and the outhouse, so she could not avoid them.

In the beginning she was rather afraid of them She thought the sounds of raised voices from the other house were dangerous arguments and feared murder was imminent but, in time, she came to understand that raised voices were normal and speaking one's mind forcefully was a way of life for the happy Bazzina family. Elena knew nothing of the protocol that passed for good manners at *Inverrigan* but was so friendly that May soon lost her reserve.

This was a happy arrangement for May, as kind-hearted Elena, recognising how ignorant May was at keeping house, took the young woman under her wing and helped her get through the first weeks. She introduced May to the many skills needed to become a good wife, including cooking good wholesome food. Soon they were friends, constantly in and out of each other's houses.

As they worked Elena kept up a constant chatter.

'When we come to Australia, Temi wanted to be farmer. The men in his family, they had all work on the wharfs in Valletta for centuries. He wants to own a bit of land and grow vegetables. We work very hard, save enough money to get deposit, buy a house with a little bit of land, but just when his dream was about to become true, Depression came. No money, no work and me with three little ones. It was dreadful time. We lost everything we had saved for. Just managed to survive. Temi, he tramp all over the country, doing anything so we could eat. His dream was gone. But God was good and times got better. We move back to Brisbane and what does he do? He works on the wharfs.' She rested her hands on her back and laughed. 'One good thing he learn during those days, how to drive. So now he drives a truck.'

May compared Elena to some of her former friends. She knew more about Elena and her family in one week than she knew about them even though they had talked for years. She realised the superficiality of those relationships. They were supposed to be friends but even their confidences had been carefully scripted to impress. For the first time in her life she could speak without first self-censoring her words and she knew that advice was not meant as criticism.

May was wearing a floral dress with padded shoulders, buttoned front and a pleated skirt that reached just below her knees. She had used precious coupons to buy it earlier in the year, but that was before she had become a housewife.

'That's pretty dress,' Elena said enviously as she fingered the rayon.

'Yes, but not after a day of housework. I've got a wardrobe

full of useless day dresses and afternoon wear. I wasted money and coupons on them. Now I can't spend Willie's money on new ones.'

'No problem. I know man who will buy them from you. No coupons needed for second hand clothes. He has many customers. Do you want me to come and see what you've got?'

'Yes please, Elena. Then I can buy sensible dresses that I can work in, something loose and washable.'

The transaction took place without any fuss and with the proceeds May bought a couple of suitable cotton dresses and a wraparound apron, which she wore most of the time.

Her long curling hair was such a nuisance that she considered cutting it, but William would have none of that. She compromised by pushing it under a snood or wearing a headscarf. Soon she had so transformed herself that she looked like any other housewife in the area and would not be recognised by those who, a short time ago, had called themselves her friends.

The new clothes had another advantage. As they were loose she could leave off her restricting corset. Her rapidly expanding breasts and waist were visible to all. There was a noticeable bump, which seemed to expand daily. Soon there was movement and William could share with her the new life growing inside.

May was at first embarrassed, then amused, that her pregnancy should become a topic of conversation with her neighbours. Not only Elena but Temi and the children would ask how the baby was going and what sex they wanted. Temi and the boys all wanted a male but Elena and little Angelina hoped it would be a baby girl.

'All children are from God,' Elena told her, 'but a girl, she is a special blessing. Boys will grow up, get married and go their own way, but a daughter will stay close to your heart all her life.'

May thought of her own daughter. They would never be close. Would she even remember her mother at all? Flora had never really been hers. Douglas and Jessica had claimed her from the start. She had been pushed to the background, the pretty lady, called Mummy, who was only present during happy times. She had rarely held her after breast feeding finished, knew nothing about teething problems, night crying or child fevers. It was only recently, when Flora had begun putting words together, that she had become a real person in May's mind. Just when they might have form a bond it had been shattered. Now she must not think of her. She must never even say her name.

She made a vow that, boy or girl, this child would be hers. Nobody would come between them. She would give this child all the love she was capable of giving.

'When your baby due?' Elena asked one day as they shared a cuppa during a break in their daily routine.

'Oh, March, I think.' May had not given a thought to the date but she knew she had missed her July period.

'You think? What does doctor say?'

'Doctor? I haven't been to see one yet.' Again, this hadn't crossed her mind. Jessica had organised everything last time and they had used the family doctor, a friend of Douglas.

'But you must see doctor. See that everything is all right, down there I mean, especially for first baby.'

May realised that Elena didn't know about Flora. Should she tell her or not? She had promised herself that she would never lie again, but was keeping quiet a lie? She had no time to analyse this though, as Elena continued.

'You must see Dr Martin tomorrow. He's good doctor. He will take care of you. I'll take you there tomorrow. Then you must book into hospital.'

'The hospital, why?'

'To have your baby. It's the safe way. Better than old midwives. They think woman should suffer. At the hospital they give you things to ease the pain and if things go wrong they just put you to sleep and pull baby out.'

Remembering the last hour of Flora's birth, May thought this a good idea. She would discuss it with Willie.

True to her word, Elena took her to see Dr Martin the next day. May was surprised to be ushered into a room full of people, mostly women. They sat on chairs placed around the room, waiting for their names to be called. May had never been to a doctor's surgery in her life. The few times she, or any other member of the household had needed his services, Dr Rivers always came to the house.

Elena spoke to a frowning, middle-aged woman who sat at a desk.

'Hello, Sister. This is Mrs Forbes. She wants to see Doctor Martin.'

'Does she have an appointment?' The woman looked down at the ledger open in front of her.

'No. She just moved in. This is her first time.'

'Does she speak English?'

Elena laughed. 'Of course she does. She's Australian.'

'Then you can sit down and she can give me her details.'

May was indignant, for Elena, at the rudeness of this woman, but her friend did not seem to be worried by it.

The sister opened the ledger in front of her. 'So, Mrs Forbes, is it?'

Until that moment May had not thought of herself as Mrs Forbes. She and Elena had been on first name terms from the beginning. This would be the first time that she had used the name our loud. She wasn't really Mrs Forbes. Legally she was still Mrs Henderson. Would she be breaking the law? She nodded in assent, conscious of another unspoken lie. Would it never end? But she was determined never to use the name Henderson again. She would ask Willie about it tonight.

'And why do you want to see Dr Martin?'

May opened her arms to show the obvious. 'I'm having a baby.'

'Yes. I can see that.' The woman's abrupt manner was unnerving May. If she had been on her own she would have left.

'But why do you want to see Doctor. Are there complications?' May turned to Elena for help.

'She has come for first check-up.' Elena called from her seat. Every head in the room looked up. May could feel herself blushing.

'Well, Doctor's book is full.' She looked at May's protruding stomach. 'But I suppose I could squeeze you in, but you will have a long wait.' She looked down the page and wrote May's name at the end of a long list.

May whispered her thanks then stumbled back to a seat beside Elena who patted her hand and whispered. 'She's like that to everybody. If she had her way no one would get to see her precious doctor.'

When her name was at last called, May walked into the room, filled with trepidation, but Dr Martin turned out to be a cheery, middle-aged man who quickly put her at her ease.

The examination, though embarrassing, was performed professionally.

'Everything seems to be in order, Mrs Forbes. The baby's heart has a strong beat and it is quite active. Your estimation is correct. I will give you a note for the hospital. We will book you in for mid-March. Make an appointment with Sister Porter and I will see you in November.'

May was alarmed. 'Why? Is something wrong?'

'No, no. Everything is fine but these days we like to keep an eye on our mothers just to see that everything is progressing well. Did this not happen last time?'

She shook her head. Of course he would know.

'And everything went well?'

She nodded.

'Are you worried about the fees?'

'No, no it is just . . .' She was about to say that last time, but then that would mean she had to explain all about Flora and how that pregnancy had gone.

'Then I shall see you in a month's time.' He was already looking at the next folder on his desk. She had been dismissed.

Willie was pleased when May told him about the visit. 'I should have thought about it myself. I'm afraid I don't know anything about childbirth May.'

'I don't think any man who isn't a doctor does, Darling. It's scary and messy. Men prefer to wait till it is over. Then they accept all the congratulations. It is the way it has always been.

193

CHAPTER 35

As May struggled through her daily toils she longed for the pampered life she had led during her first pregnancy. Still she would not change her new life with Willie for one day of it. As she eased her aching back against her open palms, she consoled herself with thoughts of Willie's gentleness, his expressions of love and the little acts he did to make her life easier. She already knew that he was willing to give his life for her. Now she knew that he would give her every day of his future too.

The months went by, measured mostly by her expanding waist and protruding stomach, but apart from heartburn and the inconvenience of constant use of the under-bed chamber pot, they passed without incident. The 9th of March was no different to any other day, but about 11p.m., getting up once to again ease her bladder, she was horrified to discover a flow of blood.

This was not how it had happened last time!

'Willie,' she screamed, 'something is wrong. Get Elena.'

William sprang from the bed, took one look at the blood and, in nothing but pyjama bottoms, pounded on the Bazzina's door shouting, 'Elena, Elena, come at once. May is bleeding to death.'

Elena, in nightdress and bare feet, opened the door, pushed William aside and ran to May's bedroom.

Temi, eyes still half closed and rubbing his hand through his thick curly hair staggered to the door demanding, 'What's–a–matta', and followed William who was racing back to his own house.

Elena took in the scene in one glance. 'It's all right my darling. It's all right,' and held the shaking May in her arms. Seeing the two men at the door, she began giving orders. 'You,' she pointed to William, 'You, get a warm rug from the bed then go, get towels from bathroom, You' she ordered Temi, 'Go back, wake Andy tell him to look after the kids then get the truck and wait for us.'

'But, where we goin'?'

'Don't ask questions. Go.'

She pointed at him and he fled. He knew who gave the orders at home.

The authority in her voice calmed May. She ceased shaking and responded sensibly as Elena found and collected the things she had prepared for her hospital stay.

When they reached the hospital, it was Elena who spoke to the duty nurse. While she examined May the nurse spoke so calmly, joking that May was clever to come at a time when there were no other mothers needing her attention, that May was sure everything would be well.

The nurse came out to let them know that everything was well. With that good report, William was dismissed. Birthing was woman's business. A frightened father would only get in the way.

Dr Martin visited her early next day and assured her that the baby was doing fine. Soon after, labour pains began and, though not too severe, progressed slowly. As the day progressed Dr

Martin became a little worried so, to save complications, May was sedated and a healthy baby boy was delivered at 3p.m.

May held the precious bundle to her and it nuzzled into her breast. His head was a little misshapen due to his manner of arrival but to May, he was the most beautiful baby that had ever been born. She would have resisted when he was taken from her but was told that she needed rest.

'He will be in the nursery with all the other babies. We will bring him to you when he needs feeding. You must get rest and make lots of milk for him to grow strong.'

'But, my husband, where is he?'

'He'll be here at visiting time. We will show him his son when he comes.'

May just had time to compare the difference to Flora's arrival, before she fell into a dreamless sleep.

Because of the stitches and the loss of blood it was seven days before May was allowed out of bed. The hours of the day was measured by feeding times when her baby was brought to her, talking with the other mothers in the ward, Elena's daily visit and the hour each evening when Willie was permitted to visit. They had not settled on a name before the birth so each evening she would greet him with a list of names, some suggested by the other women or staff. They finally settled on Robert John, for no other reason than they felt they went well with Forbes.

'It has a ring of authority,' William suggested. 'I think, with a name like that he could become someone who could give or follow orders without favour. I will start an account so that there will be money for his education.'

'Willie, he is only a baby. It will be years before he will go to school.'

'Only five years, my dear. He can spend his primary years at a state school but to get ahead it will be better if he does his secondary education at one of the colleges. I had private tutoring myself so am not an "old boy". All we can hope is that, by the time he reaches that age, the gossip will be forgotten.'

'Willie, please don't talk about that.'

He did his best to console her but the thought that the scandal would scar his son's life was never far from his mind. He might have been reduced to a common labourer but he wanted better things for his son. As he peddled around the Brisbane streets, sweating in the sun or drenched in tropical showers, he vowed he would make a better life for Robert.

Temi's truck was again commandeered to bring mother and baby home. Elena had organized a celebratory meal and Angelina immediately appointed herself Robert's nursemaid. The boys would have to wait till he was older before they could introduce him to boy's games.

Robert was a happy, healthy baby. William and May saw him as the crowning glory to their relationship. They could not call it a marriage as May was still Douglas' wife in law but, in the world in which they mixed, they were Mr and Mrs Forbes. They were not the only ones living in such a situation The law even had a name for it, *sui iuris.* It was only when filling out official documents that it became an issue. Such a document was Robert's birth certificate which read, Father: William John Forbes, Mother: May Margaret Swann.

If May had thought herself busy before, she now felt twenty-four hours was not enough to accomplish everything that had to be done. If it had not been for the help of her neighbours she was sure she would not have survived the first few months. Gradually she learned to prioritise. Robert was a healthy baby and William was the best of husbands and in time exhaustion became mere tiredness that could be cured by a good night's sleep.

Nevertheless she found the early days of motherhood exhausting. Robert seemed to need all her attention but there was still cooking, cleaning and washing that had to be done.

She did not remember Flora's babyhood being that way. It had hardly interrupting her social life. Mother took care of that, she thought. My job was done when I had produced the child. She had done all the mothering. No wonder it was so easy for me to give up Flora. It will be different this time. I don't care how hard it gets, Robert will always be my first priority and I will give my life before letting anyone take him from me.

William could see May's tiredness and tried to be of more help but at the end of a long day of pedalling his heavy, awkward bicycle around the streets of Brisbane all he wanted to do was eat and sleep.

There were times when May felt herself a failure but, with the help of the Bazzina family, she managed. She would consult Elena over every minor medical problem and Angelina appointed herself the baby's nursemaid. Only meals, school and bedtime could drag her from her duties. Temmi even jokingly accused May of kidnapping his daughter and suggested she adopt her.

CHAPTER 36

Douglas was satisfied that the scandal was now yesterday's news. He had kept his emotions intact, going about his daily business as if nothing had happened. Of course he had dropped subtle hints that anyone who assisted in William Forbes' career would no longer be looked on favourably by him or his associates but, apart from that warning, he seemed indifferent to the whole episode.

With no new gossip to fan the flame created by May's revelation in court, the fire soon burned out. The war had turned in favour of the Allies so good news headlines were the order of the day. Nobody was interested in yesterday's scandal.

When no new evidence of Gerard's likely murderer surfaced, the police lost interest and eventually it became a cold case, not forgotten but consigned to a file, to be opened only if new evidence were found. Several important persons breathed a sigh of relief.

Douglas now felt it was time he did something about creating a personal fortune that he could leave to his daughter. He had kept in contact with Hermas Vandermeer and been inspired by the man's vision of the future.

'There are acres and acres of land there Douglas, areas as big as a country just crying out for cattle.'

'But I heard the industry was in chaos because of Argentina.'

'Yes, but that is the European market. England and such. I'm talking about Asia. There's an enormous market just waiting to be tapped and I know how to deal with them. I have contacts. I have influence. All I need is someone who knows about the agricultural industry and running cattle stations. A man like you, Douglas. But we must be quick. I'm not the only one who can read the future. There are stations abandoned during the threatened invasion going for a song now. But not for long. We must buy land before post war money comes pouring back in.'

Douglas was impressed but he did his own homework and had come to believe the Hermas knew what he was talking about. Eventually they came to an understanding. Hermas would provide the finance and he would provide the knowledge and expertise. He could see himself following in his father's footsteps. He would be, not a sheep king, but a cattle baron.

The war was going so well that he felt that it would not be seen as desertion to resign his commission. He spoke with important people about his dream and was given advice and introductions to help him in his investigations of cattle breeds. Armed with these and a number of addresses, given in return for the hospitality experienced at *Inverrigan*, he organised an extended holiday in the United States and Britain.

'Jess, you'd better start packing. We're going State Side.

'State side? What do you mean Douglas?'

'State Side, woman. The good old U.S. of A.'

'You mean America?'

'Of course I mean America. Where else?'

'But Douglas, there is a war on.'

'Not for much longer. We've got the little Nips on the run. Any day now we'll be knocking on Tojo's front door. Don't know why he doesn't surrender so we can get back to fixing the world. Germany's had it. There'll be peace in Europe before you know it. If it wasn't for that maniac Hitler it would have been over years ago.'

'But Douglas, why . . .?'

'Enough with the buts and whys, Jess. You, Flora and I are leaving Australia on the 10th of March and sailing, courtesy of the United States government, to San Fran Cisco so you'd better start packing.'

He marched out of the room, mightily pleased with himself, leaving behind a bewildered Jessica. What did it all mean? She had never been anywhere, except for holidays by the sea at Sandgate. What on earth was she supposed to pack for a sea voyage to the other side of the world, especially for a growing four year old? She would need new clothes, but were there enough coupons

Jessica would have liked to shut herself in her room and have a good cry but she was so used to being at Douglas' beck and call that she immediately got a pad and paper and began making lists.

The ship, a converted cruiser returning wounded American soldiers, was hardly a luxury liner but, as Douglas had only known troop ships and the one short cruise to New Zealand and Jessica and Flora had never been to sea, they thought it the height of luxury. It took Jessica a couple of days to get her sea legs but after that she revelled in the first holiday she had had in her life. There was nothing she had to do, nowhere she had to go and the only decision she had to make was what to have for lunch and dinner.

'This is what life might have been,' she whispered to herself.

Even Douglas was overwhelmed by the size, the noise and the energy they experienced from the moment they set foot on American soil. For the first time in his life Douglas felt like a country cousin. It irritated him that everyone he spoke to seemed to believe that America had been the saviour of the civilized world.

'From Australia?' they would say. 'We certainly saved you from those Japs. We've got them on the run now. We're cleaning up those Huns, beat them on the beaches and now we're rolling them up one town at a time. They'll be begging for peace any day soon.'

Douglas had been brought up to be polite to those offering hospitality but he let off steam when alone with Jessica.

'As if they were the only ones fighting this war. Granted they are doing a good job and it would have taken us years by ourselves, but where were they at the beginning? Who was it held the line in New Guinea? If the Japs had taken Port Moresby Australia would have gone faster than a bag of chips and then where would McArthur and his men have set up camp? Anyway they were lousy fighters, so I hear. It was their superior weaponry that made the difference.'

'Then we can only be thankful that they have it,' Jessica replied. She was not as confident as Douglas or her American hosts. She would not believe that war was ended until she heard peace bells ringing.

However much he was annoyed by their boasting it did not stop Douglas from joining in the celebrations when Germany surrendered in May.

Apart from their predisposition to boast, Douglas loved everything about America and Americans, their confidence in the future, their "get up and go" attitude and the philanthropy of the wealthy class. There was no "old country" to be looking back to. No wonder they were streets ahead of Australia. They were the people of tomorrow.

There had always been cattle on Lochaber and the other stations, but only as a sideline. Now he had to become an expert, especially of the breeds that would do best in the north. He knew the qualities of the red-coated Herefords and black Angus breeds but now he was learning of Brahmans and the Bos indictus. He felt he would never come to admire their musculo-fatty hump and pendulous dewlap but he was assured that they had a tolerance to both heat and ticks.

'I suppose I won't be breeding them for their looks,' he remarked.

He also met ranchers who were experimenting with new cross breeds and spent many an evening drinking Jim Bean and planning how he would import semen and fertilised ova.

Flora blossomed during her time in America. Till then she had led a rather solitary life, Jessica, Rosa and Beppi being her only companions. She had sometimes been brought out to be introduced to Douglas' friends or paraded around at May's garden parties, but she had met few children her own age.

Mixing mainly with adults, she had a vocabulary far beyond

her years, which enchanted the people she now came in contact with. They loved her accent and expressed surprise at her ability to hold her own in conversation.

Flora gloried in the attention. She became quite precocious, ignoring Jessica's frowns and mild reprimands. It was no good complaining to Douglas. She was his daughter and she could do no wrong.

'After all, one day she will inherit the empire I am creating for her. She will have to hold her own against all comers. She is learning how to fulfil her role just as I am learning mine.'

Jessica kept her own council about that, as she did about most things these days. She wondered when the woman she once was had become this person, "Jess", a glorified servant to Douglas and his daughter, at their beck and call. Still she had had a choice. She could have left with May. But a life without Flora would have been worse than death. The life she now led was the cost she had to pay to be close to her granddaughter and to watch her grow.

They were still in America when the miracle bomb was dropped. Within a few days the war was over. August 14th in America, 15th in Australia, saw the end of the worst war in the history of mankind and the beginning of what everyone believed would be the end to all wars. Now that they had the ultimate weapon that could destroy whole cities with one bomb, no one would challenge them. Disputes would be settled by negotiation and the world would know peace and prosperity for all.

CHAPTER 37

POST WAR

They arrived in England a week before Christmas. For the first time they saw the devastation that war could bring. It had been one thing to see it all on newsreels, but the reality shocked them. Whole neighbourhoods lay in ruins. How could anyone have lived through it and where could they find the courage to start again?

The war was over but rationing was still a part of daily life. Queuing for food was an everyday necessity and food served, even in the best of restaurants was questionable. They had to search the menus to find anything that was edible

'I do not like it here, Jess. I want to go back to America' Flora complained.

'But we must have Christmas in London,' Jessica consoled her.

'But they do not even have proper Christmas pudding.'

Douglas found the English no less confusing than the Americans. 'They're so bloody cheerful,' Douglas complained. 'They walk around with smiles on their faces and they happily stand for hours and hours queuing for this disgusting muck they call food. I know they had to put up with it during the war but that's been over nearly six months. I think they've been keeping the "stiff upper lip" for so long it's become normal to them. How anyone can cheerfully sit down to this and call it a good meal is beyond me. Can't even get a proper egg. Hope it's better in Scotland.'

Douglas had been looking forward to his first Hogmanay but the cold of London was   getting into his bones and he knew it would be worse further north. They travelled by train to Edinburgh, where Douglas had relatives on his mother's side. The warmth of their greeting more than compensated for the cold outside.

Jeanie had corresponded regularly during her lifetime and her letters had inspired her stay-at-home relatives. Even the following generation knew about Aunty Jeanie, who left her home in Scotland to take the long sea voyage to a strange new land to marry her childhood sweetheart. It had become a family legend.

They were anxious to confirm the stories she had written of her life at the other end of the world. They could hardly believe that one family could own so much land. Douglas exhausted himself answering their questions.

'Were there no savage animals?' they asked and were amazed to find that kangaroos ate only grass.

'Had there been many wars before they subdued the natives?'

'There were not many of them,' he explained, 'and they had no concept of land. They used to wander over it, eating what they found. Father had some trouble at first as they thought they could just take a sheep when they wanted one, but we've tamed them. Now some of them work on the stations and the rest have been rounded up by the authorities and live on reservations.

There are some wild ones way out west, but only anthropologists and missionaries go there. They're a dying race really, so we are making their passing as easy as possible.'

They stayed a week while Douglas mapped out a route that would take them to the highlands and the land of his ancestors, north to Glencoe and Fort William then on to the fabled Island of Skye. But before the journey began Flora was coughing and running a temperature so he left her in Jessica's care in Edinburgh and continued on alone.

He was pleased to be on his own, on this journey that he had dreamed of taking all his life. As he neared the places his father had spoken of, he felt an almost religious fervour. He was like a medieval pilgrim. He had heard the stories over and over. Now he felt a part of them.

Finally he arrived at the sacred site at Glencoe. It had loomed so large in his imagination he had expected to find substantial buildings, majestic monuments. Instead there was a silent, green glen, a willow-the-wisp fog, purple mountains and majestic peaks. A path led up to a tall, thin, grey Celtic cross atop a rocky cairn on which was a simple inscription

Erected in memory of the chief of the MacDonald clan who fell with his people at the massacre of Glencoe

Douglas stood, silent. In his mind he could hear the cries and the curses of the defenceless clan. The words - *who fell with his people* - echoed in his head. He fell to his knees, tears running down his cheeks. He had been transported back in time. He was beside his chief and he would die beside him.

After a time Douglas came to himself. He still felt disoriented but knew that he had lived through something he could never explain, but he would retain the experience of it for the rest of his life.

While Douglas was experiencing this occurrence, the weather, which had already been unpleasant, worsened. A cruel wind blew down from the mountains and a dusting of snow fell on the ground and his shoulders. He tried to stand but his legs would not obey him. For a fleeting moment he thought he would die here among his ancestors. He crawled to the edge of the monument and pulled himself up. Feeling much older than his fifty-two years he walked slowly back to his hired car. He turned on the heater and sat for some time until he felt sufficiently thawed to begin his journey. He spent the night at Fort William but still felt unwell next morning so decided he would cancel the rest of his planned trip, go back to London and then sail for Australia as soon as he could get a berth.

When he reached Edinburgh he was running a temperature. Jessica argued he should take to his bed but he insisted they catch the train to London. He sat in a corner of the compartment, a red, green and blue tartan shawl across his shoulders, coughing, blowing and sipping on good Scotch whisky.

Flora, somewhat recovered, could hardly recognize her ailing father.

'Is he going to die, Jess?' she whispered. She knew all about death. That was when you went to heaven and never came back again. Her mother was in heaven. Perhaps her father was going to visit her?

'I don't want him to go to heaven too.'

'He is not going to leave us, darling. He has a nasty cold, like you had.'

Jessica consoled the child but was, herself, afraid. What if he did die? What would happen to them alone in a strange country?

By the time they reached the capital Douglas was so ill that the next day he was admitted to the Royal London Hospital. He had pneumonia and, for three days hovered between life and death. In his delirium he drove mobs of cattle forward only be to be stopped again and again by flooding rivers.

Finally the fever broke but he was so weakened that the doctor recommended a month's rest.

During his convalescence he received a letter from Vandermeer.

My dear Douglas, it began. *When are you coming home? I have found the perfect property. It was destocked and abandoned during the war but not all the stock were rounded up and now there are cattle, some say a hundred or more, who have survived and multiplied over the years. Think man, what wonderful animals they will be. They are practically native. What wonderful stock to breed with your imports.*

It is an established station, homestead, outbuildings etc. and has a permanent water supply. The owners wish to settle down south so are anxious to sell. We could get a real bargain. I would put my own money into it, but first I am not from this country and, because of that fiend Sukarno and his KNIP who are making it so difficult with their revolutionary activities to return to Java at this present time, I have no ready capital.

My friend, this opportunity will not last. Could you contact your bank and arrange for money to cover a loan for the present to cover the first mortgage payment. As soon as things settle down here I will rearrange all my assets and take over the loan. I am only asking because I know this bargain will be snapped up if we do not act immediately.

I will forward the contract and all relevant information as soon as you agree.

His rational mind knew that what he had experienced during his illness had been part of his delirium, but he wanted to believe it had been a message from his Chief. When the letter arrived he saw it as confirmation of his destiny. He was to go forward with his enterprise.

Had Douglas been back in Australia he would never have rushed into such an arrangement, but he was still weak from his illness, homesick for the southern sun and still bewitched by his Glencoe experience. He saw himself founding a new empire, making a name for himself, a true son of Clan Eanruig. He spent hours making trunk calls to his bank, then fretted at the time wasted before he could sail for home.

The sea voyage and warmer climes restored Douglas to health. By the time they arrived in Brisbane he was impatient to begin his new adventure. He was not deterred by the reality he found. The property, rather than being destocked because of the threat of invasion had, in fact, been abandoned during the depression and had been on the market for years. There were no prospective customers waiting in the wings but rather a disillusioned pastoral company only too willing to sell. Both his bank and some of his friends advised caution, but Douglas had a dream and would not listen. Even when Hermas, his former wealth devastated through war, reluctantly pulled out, Douglas persisted.

By then he had seen, first hand, that *Arrandale* was little more than undeveloped land. To call the main building a homestead, was a fiction. It was no more than a large, dilapidated structure, some of it open to the elements. The outbuildings and fences were broken and the property was overrun with dingoes, donkeys and wild goats. The cattle had been roaming unhindered for so long that any residual memory of domesticity was gone. They were as wild as when the species had first encountered man.

But, where others saw disaster, Douglas saw only opportunity. He reasoned that when Ewan Henderson had walked onto his future empire there had been nothing. Surely, with all the advantages of modern roads, transport and communication, his son could do the same.

He remembered his father as a man in his middle forties. He forgot that when Ewan had first founded his empire he was nearer to twenty.

Douglas saw himself as a young man astride his horse, riding the boundaries of his vast domain, undisputed ruler of all he surveyed. In fact he was over fifty and had not ridden for years. He quickly compromised by buying a war surplus jeep and contemplated getting a pilot's licence. The property, *Arrandale*, had an untamed beauty about it and permanent water, but the soil was poor and the native grass of little nutritious value, so unlike the lush pastures of the Darling Downs.

Douglas' plan had been that, as soon as he had *Arrandale* up and running, he would spend his time between it and *Inverrigan*, leaving the day-to-day running to a manager, but he was finding it difficult to employ a reliable man. He also had difficulty securing good stockmen and relied heavily on Willie Nallak, a half-caste, whose family were native to the surrounding area. Had he been white, Douglas would have made him manager, but he had no book learning and white stockmen would object to taking orders from a black.

Over the years Douglas hired a number of white managers but most turned out to be unreliable, and those who were, quickly realised that *Arrandale* would never be a successful run, and moved to greener pastures. Consequently Douglas spent more and more time away from Brisbane and Flora.

He tried to be home for her birthday and, as time went on, found more and more reasons to fly back to Brisbane. He would never have admitted it to himself but he was getting too old for the life he had chosen. It was only at *Inverrigan* that he could relax. Only there could he believe his dream would succeed.

CHAPTER 38

Douglas knew that he was getting too old for a life as a pioneer. Sometimes, after a particularly hard day he would admit to himself that his venture was a failure. He should have just walked away, but the dream persisted. It must have been even harder for his father in the early days he would tell himself.

It was only his respites an *Inverrigan* that gave him the strength to go on. With the first sight of his home he could feel his spirits lifting and embracing his beloved daughter made it all worthwhile. He was doing it for her.

Douglas' favourite place of relaxation was on the veranda. That it had been William who designed it did not disturb him. He preferred the riverside for there always seemed to be a cooling breeze coming off the water. Today he was entertaining one of his oldest friends, Albert Reid. They sat in cane chairs, whiskies resting on a small table within arm's reach. They had been discussing the recent cricket match between Australia and the West Indies, which had ended in a draw.

Flora did not disturb them but curled up on the cane lounge intending to read *Captain Jim,* the last of the Billabong books, but after a few pages her eyes grew heavy and the voices of her father and Mr Reid lulled her into a halfway state, somewhere between awake and sleep.

Albert Reid stood up, walked to the edge, leant on the rail and looked towards the Brisbane River.

'This is a wonderful view, Douglas. I think you have the best position in the area. You were a clever fellow to add the veranda. When you first mentioned it I thought it would spoil the architectural style but it blends in perfectly.'

'I do a lot of my thinking here.' Douglas picked up his glass and took a sip.

'I miss it when I go north. I have a great waterhole with a waterfall up there. The view would rival this and I intend building the new homestead there as soon as the station begins to make serious money. I will have a wide veranda all round just like this.'

Albert turned back towards his friend. 'One would never know that it had been added on. Good architect. William Forbes wasn't it?'

'Yes, the scoundrel.'

Flora heard the anger in her father's voice.

Douglas stood, threw the rest of the whisky down his throat, and joined his friend at the rail.

Albers realised he had spoken without thinking. 'I'm sorry, Douglas. I forgot.'

'No Albert, no need to apologize. Water under the bridge these days. But it still rankles. I invited the bastard into the house in the first place. I admit that, after it happened, I was tempted to pull the whole thing down but then I thought, bugger it, he may have designed it but I'm the one who can enjoy it. Glad now that I saw sense.'

'Never heard from him again. Any idea where he is?'

'In Hell, if there is any justice. Took what he could then slunk away like the cur he was.' Then changing the subject to cricket. 'Did you get to see that last delivery?'

Flora heard the change of tone and knew her father was himself again.

'Yes, and I swear I'll never see a better throw again. Hit middle stump. It wasn't a luck throw, you know. That was sheer talent. A draw was a just result.'

Flora could relax. They were back on a safe topic. She loved her father with all her heart, missed him when he was away up north, and though only ten, went out of her way to make his visits home as happy as possible. She wished he would take her with him when he left, but he would say that the present homestead was not fit for a young girl but, when he built the new one, he would fly her up there in style and she would be its queen. She would be the most beautiful young woman in all of Queensland.

'In the meantime, Miss, you have got to work hard at your studies and listen to Jess. She knows how to run a house. I'll have to come and see if you are as good on a horse as you say. You will need to be a competent horsewoman up there.'

The conversation between her father and Mr Reid had worried her so that evening she asked Jessica. 'Jess, who was William Forbes?'

Jessica was so shocked that she almost dropped the book she was reading. 'Where did you hear that name?'

'Mr Reid and Father were speaking of him. Father said he was a scoundrel.'

'It was all a long time age, Flora, but I wouldn't speak of it to your father. It might stir up unpleasant memories.'

'Did Forbes cheat on him or something?'

'Flora, listen to me. All these events happened so long ago, but speaking of them can still hurt. Remember there are always two sides to every story. Nobody knows it all. Just believe me. Nobody will be any the better for digging up the past. Your father has put it behind him and so should you. Promise me that you will never mention that name again.'

Flora sensed that Jess was deadly serious. 'I promise, Jess. I won't say anything about it again.'

But though she kept her promise she remembered the name, and after her father had lost his fortune she convinced herself that William Forbes was one of the villains who had destroyed him.

Douglas persisted, year after year, using up all his personal wealth and dipping into the Henderson fortune, but not once in ten years, did the station made a profit. At first he had tried to divide his time between *Arrandale* and *Inverrigan* but that proved impossible. He had installed managers but none saw his vision or were prepared to devote their lives to someone else's dream. Eventually he had to admit failure and retired, still in debt to the banks, a broken man. He died in 1959, just as Flora was expecting to become a valued member of the society she had grown up in.

It was only with his death that the extent of Douglas' borrowing became known. He was not only bankrupt but heavily in debt. The empire he had dreamed of leaving to his daughter had never eventuated. *Inverrigan* had to be sold to cover the debts he had incurred.

Charles and his family were not all that sad to relinquish a property to which they had never had a close affinity but Flora was devastated. She refused to believe that her father had died penniless. She chose to believe that it had been a diabolical plot, devised by Uncle Charles.

She also remembered the conversation she had heard between Father and Mr Reid. What was the name, Forbes or something? Her father had called him a cur. She had almost forgotten but now she remembered him saying that the man had taken all that he could get. It was one of the few times that she could remember her father speaking angrily of someone.

Jess had given her an ambiguous answer when she had asked her about the man, which was typical of her. She always saw the best in everyone. That was probably because she had led such as easy life in the Henderson household. She would find life different now that she didn't have Father to protect her.

Jess had said it was old history and it would upset her father to refer to it. So it must have been something dreadful.

Now she realised that this Forbes character must have had something to do with her father's financial troubles. He must have been in cahoots with the dastardly relatives. She added his name to her black list.

'How dare they accuse Father? Everyone knows that he was the most honourable of men. Uncle Charles has never liked *Inverrigan*. He's only selling it for spite.'

Jessica, who had secretly been worried for some time, tried to placate her granddaughter. 'May, your father had not been a well man for some time. Perhaps his judgement...'

'His judgement? How dare you suggest that my father was

not in full control of his faculties? Next thing you will be saying that he was senile. How could you? After all he has done for you?'

Jessica was so used to swallowing insults that she ignored this one. 'May, let us not quarrel. Things are not so bad. Your Aunt Molly suggested that she could buy one of those apartments further down the street and we could live in it. They are very fashionable, you know.'

'How very gracious of her. Put the poor relative in a flat and then bask in the praise of being such a good Christian. No thank you. I will not take charity from anyone. I will make my own way.'

'But what will you do?'

'Do? I have already done it. I have applied for a position in a prestigious school in Adelaide. I read about it in *Outback Magazine.* I hope to leave here before Christmas.'

'Leave here? But where will we live?'

'I will live in at Alexandra Ladies Academy. What you intend to do with yourself I neither know nor care. Perhaps you can throw yourself on the mercies of the family. After all, you have served them for long enough. Perhaps they will take pity on you.'

Inverrigan became a private hospital where Jessica worked for many years. She spent the last of her years in a retirement village, the fees for which had been arranged by Molly, who alone recognised the years of service she had given to Douglas and his family.

CHAPTER 39

With the end of the war Australia entered a new period of change and prosperity. Population increased, due largely to migration. New industries opened and new ideas began to filter through society.

As William rode the streets of Brisbane he observed the post war rebuilding that he had hoped to be part of when he had been at Drivers. He became resigned to the fact that he would never again work in the field he loved but still kept abreast with new trends.

New suburbs were being developed, including large public housing estates to provide homes for the European Reffos and Ten Pound Poms who were migrating to Australia. The cost and speed of their erection was made possible by a new building material, Fibrolite. External, internal and ceilings could all be made from this new material and, when painted, no one would guess that they were sheets of grey asbestos-cement.

William thought that the designs left a lot to be desired but they were an excellent way to house a large number of people quickly.

Life had changing in other ways. Women had had a taste of freedom. They wanted more, and one way they could express their growing independence was in their dress. They had put up with the austerity dress during the war years with their square shoulders and short, tight skirts. Many had spent their teen years in uniform. They wanted something softer, more feminine and *Christian Dior* gave it to then. It was called the New Look, long sweeping skirts with fitted waists and rounded shoulders or tailored suit coats with peplum and fitted calf length skirts. When first seen on the streets of Brisbane they caused some disparaging remarks but within months every woman had to have one.

Fashion had played a vital part in May's former life, even as a child. She had been given a toy sewing machine that really worked and, in no time, she was designing and making clothes for her dolls, copied from illustrations she had seen in Womans Mirror, a woman's magazine of which Douglas approved of because it was produced by the Bulletin.

Later overseas magazines such as Vogue became fashion bibles for May and her friends. From these they learnt of the latest trends in Europe and America and schemed to be the first seen with the latest creations. Sometimes May copied designs she had found in these magazines and had them made for her, long before they became available in Australia. As one of the leading hostesses in Brisbane her clothing was often commented on and copied, even during wartime.

During the first few months in South Brisbane she had had little interest in clothing but, as Robert became less demanding and she regained her former figure, she began to long for an elegant, post-war dress. William heard the longing in her voice as she talked with Elena about the wonderful "New Look."

'May, we might not be wealthy, but we are not paupers. Go and buy yourself something you like,' he told her.

May knew that the dresses she desired were beyond their budget, but remembering her former talent, she played with the idea that she could buy material and make her own dresses. Elena had a Singer Sewing Machine. She could borrow it and make them herself.

She did not want to waste money so decided to experiment with dresses she already had. She took two of them to pieces then by using the material from both created a new multicoloured dress with soft round neckline, nipped in waist and a flowing, mid-calf skirt.

When it was finished she called her friend.

'Elena, what do you think?' She twirled around to display the flowing skirt. 'Does it look like the one in the picture?'

'May, it's beautiful. Like a princess would wear. And you made this from old dresses? Could you make me one too?'

The dresses created quite an impression among their neighbours. First one and then another begged May and Elena to make a dress for them too. Soon they had a little business going in the room that William had once dreamed of as an office.

May had not meant to go there but one day, having dressed Robert in a new shirt and shorts, she put on her latest creation, took especial care with her makeup, caught a tram into the city then another to Newfarm. They walked along Brunswick Street until they were opposite *Inverrigan*.

She looked across at the beautiful pink building with its lacy veranda and well-tended garden and for one moment yearned again for the life she had led there. Her eyes filled with tears.

'Mummy, why are you crying?'

May pulled herself back into the present. 'I'm not crying darling. I'm just looking at my old house and remembering.'

'You used to live there? In that big house?'

'Yes I did.'

'Can we go and have a look?'

'No Robert, I do not know the people who live there now.' She hurried him away and walked on towards the river, horrified that she could have risked being seen by a member of the household.

On the way home Robert asked, 'Can we visit the Big House again tomorrow, Mummy?'

May saw the excitement in his eyes and realised that she had exposed him to a forbidden part of her life. Why had she gone there and what would happen if he told Willie? She must stop him speaking about it.

'Robert, you are a big boy and you know what a secret is, don't you?'

'Yes, Mummy. A secret is something you never tell anybody.'

'Well, I want the Big House to be a secret between you and me. We must never speak of it again and we must never tell Daddy.'

'Why?'

'Because, because it might make him sad. It will be our special secret. Will you promise?'

'Yes Mummy.' He felt very grown up. He had a special secret with his mother that he could not share, not even with his father.

He kept his promise but began to dream about the house. The next incident happened soon after he began school. Angelina used to walk him to and from school and they often came home by way of Musgrove Park. One afternoon a well-dressed lady spoke to them and asked their names. She even gave them a penny each to spend.

Angelina had been well schooled by Elena about talking to strangers, but this was a woman and so well dressed. She knew that dangerous strangers were always men.

The lady asked if she could walk home with them. Just as they reached the front gate May happened to be coming out the front door looking for them. She had a moment of fear as she recognized Jessica and felt a wave of hatred for this woman who had robbed her of her daughter. She was not going to do the same with her son.

'Robert, Angelina. Go inside at once.'

Robert had been looking forward to introducing his mother to the nice lady but one look at his mother's stern expression and he and Angelina scuttled past her and hurried into the security of the house.

'What do you want here?' May demanded.

'Oh May, please. I do not mean any harm. I just wanted to see you and my grandson.'

May could feel the muscles on her face tighten. She folded her arms across her chest and glared at her mother.

'He is not your grandson. He is my son. You are not my mother. You rejected me once. Now I am rejecting you. If I ever see you near my son again I will report you to the police.' She turned back into the house and slammed the door.

Jessica stood in the street for some time, looking at the house where her daughter and grandson lived, then walked away, a broken woman. She had made a choice. Now she would have to live with it.

Inside, May grabbed Robert roughly by the shoulders. 'Robert, you must never speak to that woman again. If you see her you must run home to me straight away.'

'Yes, Mum, but who is she?'

'She is a wicked woman who could harm you.' May could see the look of horror in her son's eyes but, if it would keep him safe from Jessica's influence, she did not care.

Robert was a bright student, enjoyed learning and did well in tests. William and May dreamed of a bright future for him. William had already taken out a special bank account for his future education. He knew the value placed on a private school education so every week five shillings from his wages was saved to go towards Robert's future.

But one afternoon, when Robert was in grade four, he arrived home in a dishevelled state. His shirt was torn, his socks were around his ankles, his face was red and he was puffed from running.

May was shocked. 'Robert, have you been fighting?'

'Yes. With Bert Archer.' Anger was burning in his eyes.

'But why, Robert? Only rough boys fight.'

'He said that Dad killed somebody and you told a lie to get him off.'

It was like a punch in the stomach. May's world was falling down around her. She saw the anger in her son's eyes turn to confusion. She knew she must reassure him.

'Oh Robert, what a terrible thing for him to say. As if your father could hurt anyone. And do you think I would tell a lie?'

'No Mum.' But she could hear doubt in his voice. She knelt down and looked into his eyes. 'Robert, this Bert, does he often get into fights?'

He nodded his head.

'And would you say he is a bully?'

He nodded again.

'Sometimes people are not happy in themselves so they try to make others unhappy by hurting them. If they cannot do this with their fists they do it with lies. These people are not worth listening to and certainly not worth fighting with. I want you to forget the dreadful things he said and try to stay out of his way. When he sees that he cannot hurt you he will soon start tormenting someone else.'

She stood, put her arm around him and pulled him towards her. 'Now promise me that you will never listen to any evil talk about me or your father.'

Robert, forgetting for a moment that he was a big boy and big boys didn't go in for mushy things like hugs and kisses, leaned in and hugged her back. They locked together for a time gaining strength from their united love, then he stepped back, a little ashamed.

May ruffled his hair. 'My little hero.' They laughed together but as he was about to walk away she said, in an offhanded way, as if it didn't really matter, 'don't tell Daddy, darling. It might upset him.'

May had read fairy stories to Robert before he could read. To make sense of them he had woven the first two strange events into a personal story. The Big House became a castle where the beautiful maiden, May, had been kept prisoner by the wicked witch, the Nice Lady.

He was too old for fairy stories when the third event happened but, at night, in that eerie time when sleep is claiming our conscious minds, it became part of the story.

William, in his dirty, oil stained overalls and riding his black bicycle became a scary figure, sometimes under the spell of some wicked wizard, at other times was himself the evil presence who had stolen the maiden from her rightful palace. Whether he was evil or a hero, he was the cause of his mother's downfall and her banishment from the beautiful place. It was his job to protect her from harm.

Had William's health been stronger this rift might well have been healed but his lungs, which had kept him out of the war, also made him unfit for the work he was doing. By the end of a working day he would stagger into the house and sit, wheezing. May would stop whatever she was doing to give him her full attention.

Robert, knowing how hard his mother worked and not understanding the nature of William's illness, felt that he exaggerated it to claim his mother's time.

He grew closer to his mother and distant from his father. When William urged him to study harder he rebelled.

'If you were so clever why didn't you study and get a decent job?' he demanded. 'Then Mum wouldn't have to slave away all day.' He would stomp off to his bedroom and sulk until called for tea.

CHAPTER 40

When Robert was twelve William's asthma became so bad he could no longer work. Because he had been in government employ he was retired on a small pension. With the money May earned from her dressmaking they managed to get by but any thought of Robert attending a private school had gone. The money saved was spent on essentials and William's medicine. Robert began his secondary education at the local high school but in his second year William died. Robert left school as soon as he turned fourteen and began his working life. It was only with the encouragement of one of his teachers that he continued his studies at night school and completed his Q.C.E.

Such is the vagary of fate that, in the same week that May buried William, several notices in the bereavement columns of the Courier Mail announced the death of one of Brisbane's well known citizens, Douglas Ewan Henderson.

Because they had never married, May was not entitled to a widow's pension or to the proceeds of William's life insurance. This money would be Robert's when he turned eighteen.

The dressmaking, which had once been only a supplement now became the only source of income May had. It had grown into a family business. Angelina had become a competent seamstress and apprentice designer. William, during his illness and wanting to help May, had designed a large cardboard folder with an outline of all sizes from eight to twenty two. By using these templates May could make allowances for irregular body shapes so that she could design and cut dresses to fit irregular sizes. Some of the new fashions, such as the 'sack' and the 'a line' were unforgiving to larger sizes but May was able to fashion her dresses to please most of her customers.

'May,' Elena called excitedly as she came into the sewing room. 'May, you remember Mr Shein, the man who used to sell second hand clothes during the war? Well, now there's is no more rationing he's opened dress shops, not like Coles and Woolworths but real ladies' shops. Shops for rich ladies who want originals.'

'That is nice for him, but I do not think he will take our customers away.'

'No, no May. He wants to sell **our** dresses. Been watching me and he thinks we could make special dresses, just for his shops.' She laughed. 'He calls them salons. Makes the ladies think they're in Paris, he says.'

'We couldn't live on selling to one shop, Elena.'

'No, listen, I said, "shops". In Brisbane, Sydney, Melbourne, different, you know, one in every city, even Perth, he says. You make only one dress for ten shops in different places. Because they're special he can charge the earth and the ladies will pay. He says, "You make the dresses, I will sell them." He really knows what he's talking about. He's a Jew.'

'You mean, like a fashion house.' May remembered a time

when she and her friends would anxiously await the arrival of the latest overseas fashions. How important it was to be the first to be seen wearing them. 'But we are only three people. How could we sell enough to make as much money as we do now?'

'I've thought of that. We could get 'nother machine. Get two, three and employ my friends. You won't have to cut to fit all shapes and sizes. Just design and make to regular sizes. Easy.'

Not quite so easy, May thought, but fittings do take time. It would be more interesting making clothes she wanted, rather than what the customer required. Would it really succeed?

'What about material?'

'Oh, Shein will organise that. His family's in the rag trade. All you do is tell him what you want, colour, cloth, you know. He'll do the rest. He says we can have our own brand. What you think of that?'

'Our own label you mean.' May knew how a name could sell a dress.

'Yes, we call it, *May Forbes*, or something.'

'No. We will call it "*Elena*". It sounds better.'

Elena was delighted and May didn't tell her the reason why she would not use her own name. She hoped the dresses would become famous but she didn't want anyone to connect them to her. She knew the fashion world and it would only be a matter of time before someone made the connection and the scandal would be all over the papers again.

Post war Australia was changing so quickly that some feared that good old British stock would be submerged in a sea of European nationalities, from the Baltic states in the north to the Greeks and Italians in the south. But, as the Reffos. became D.P.s and eventually New Australians, they created an homogenous new identity which still retained a strong colonial flavour.

Times were good, unemployment was non-existent, many taking on more than one job, and women began to find work outside of the home. There was money for things other than essentials and clothing became an obsession with women of all walks of life. There was never a better time to be in the fashion industry.

May spent her evenings pouring over fashion magazines from all corners of the globe and from these created her own distinctive style. As skirts went up and down, pencil slim or very full, held out with lace or rope petticoats, Peter Pan necklines giving way to halter neck, shoestring and strapless, May always managed to add a little something extra. Soon *Elena* dresses were being worn by the most discerning of ladies. They more than held their own against imports from Europe and America.

Of course success brought curiosity. Fashion writers wanted to know more about the creators behind *Elena*. For some time Mr Stein, who had been told by Elena that the woman behind the designs was a lady, fallen on hard times who did not wish to be known, felt that the mystery added to the legend. But a secret can be kept for only so long. The investigating instinct is just as strong in fashion writers as in the most intrepid of news reporters.

For a time Angelina was thought to be the new genius but eventually the news broke that the brains behind *Elena* was none other than the notorious May Henderson. Reporters with cameras camped outside her modest home, T.V. presenters offered her large sums for an 'exclusive' and extracts from the trial were plastered across local and interstate newspapers.

May retreated inside her house, refusing to speak to anyone. Elena did her best to drive the reporters and curious bystanders away but they were persistent. Temi was nearly arrested for brandishing an old shotgun and threatening to shoot them if they didn't get away from his house. May's one consolation was that Willie was dead so could not relive the shame.

There were no more *Elena* creations. Four years later another line, under the name *Angelina* was launched but it never held the prestige of *Elena.*

Robert had not been neglecting his studies. While May spent her evenings in the sewing room, he spent his at the kitchen table studying towards his QCE. The Bizzina's rejoiced in the success of *Elena,* but he only saw the amount of work it meant for his mother. Only the name pleased him. Nobody could connect him to it. He could not believe that any woman would willingly spend endless hours making dresses if she had the choice. He was blind to the pleasure May got from her creations. He saw only the exhaustion at the end of a long night as she sketched her ideas on large sheets of paper. To him she was just a dressmaker and it was all his father's fault for not having provided for her. It made him even more determined to get a well-paid job so that she could retire.

Robert learnt of the sensational news about the fashion's creator from a headline he read that evening, on his way home from night school.

May Henderson

Mystery Woman Behind the Clothing Brand
Elena

He burst into the house and found his mother sitting in the kitchen, her hands around a half-drunk cup of cold tea staring into space. She was trying to come to terms with having been exposed to the public.

'Are you May Henderson?'

'What?' May was shaken out of the depressed state she was sinking into. 'What are you talking about?'

'I know that you design the dresses. Are you May Henderson?' he shouted.

'Robert, calm down.'

'Just answer me. Are you?'

May took a deep breath. She had always dreaded the time when she would have to explain her circumstances. She had thought it might have been when he saw his birth certificate. She had always thought that she would just tell him that she had been married before she met his father. She never thought it would all come out like this.

'Sit down... please.'

When he had slumped into a nearby chair she joined her hands together, placed them on the table and began. 'When I was quite young I was married to a much older man whose surname was Henderson. He was not a bad man but I did not truly love him. I had known your father for some time. He was my best friend. As I grew older I realised that what I felt for your father was more than friendship. It was love, real love, but because my husband did not divorce me your father and I could not marry.'

'I don't care whether you were married or not. Was he the

man Bert Archer told me about all those years ago? Was he the man who was on trial for murder?

'Yes, but he was found not guilty.'

'Because you lied for him. You said it wasn't true. You lied to me.'

'I did not lie, Robert.' Lies again, she thought. They always catch up with you. Lies and half lies. 'Your father did come to see me that night.'

'Why should I believe you now?'

'Because I am your mother. Your father was with me that night and I know he did not kill that man. Now please, don't speak of this again. Is it not enough that my name is in all the gossip columns? I wish that I was dead.'

She put her head into her opening hands and cried like a child. She cried for the life she had lived. She cried for her dead lover and she cried for the anger and scorn she saw in her son's eyes.

Robert was shocked. He could not remember one time in his life, even when his father had died, when his mother had not been in control of her emotions. She had always been the calm centre of his life, the rock on which his world had been built. All anger was gone as he tried to console her.

'Mum, don't cry. I'm sorry. I should never have shouted at you. I believe you Mum. I know you would never lie to me. Please forgive me.'

He put his arms around her. She turned into his embrace and slowly the crying turned to controlled sobs. In time she wiped her cheeks and looked into his face.

'Oh darling. It is not fair. You are too young to be dragged into a world of adult drama. One day I will explain it all, but for now could we not speak of it?'

'Of course Mum. I promise I will never bring it up again. Now, you sit here and I will make you another, hot cup of tea and then I will tell you what happened at work today.'

CHAPTER 41

But Robert could not leave it alone. He had to know what had gone on in her former life. His childhood fantasies returned but he tried to rationalise them now that he knew more about real life.

There had been a murder. His father had been accused. His mother's evidence had saved him but it had somehow changed her life. The 'big house' and the 'nice lady' had had something to do with it, and it had happened before he was born. If it was so sensational that it could even make news today, then it must have been in all the papers then. So he would do some research through old papers. He would take a day off work and start with the year before he was born.

He waded through 1944 headlines until he came to the first report that Gerard's death had not been an accident. This could be the one, he thought. He had to wade through several more papers before he came to the news of William being charged.

From then he read the daily report of each day of the trial. The headline "Is This Sir Galahad?" made him pause. 'Fairy stories again,' he muttered as he turned to the next day's court report, but he didn't have to look beyond the first page. "Sensational News in Reid Murder" the headlines screamed and there was his mother's image, large as life, staring back at him from the Tribune, above the words *"wife of prominent pastoralist and member of the Ministry of Food."*

He closed his eyes and took a deep breath. So it was all true? When he opened them again he happened to notice the date at the head of the paper, *16th October.*

He thumped his fists on the reading table and shouted, 'No.' then, realising that he was in a public place, took breaths until he had some control then stood and walked out of the reading room. Once outside he sank onto a convenient bench and put his head in his hands, trying to process the information he had just learnt.

If he was born in April of 1945 that meant she must have been pregnant when she gave her evidence? Even if he had been born premature, which no one had ever said he was, she would still have to have been already a little bit pregnant at the time.

Which meant that she and his father must have been carrying on an affair while she was still married. The news revolted him. How could his mother have done such a terrible thing? How could he ever face her again, now that he knew? Perhaps William was not his father after all? No, that was not true. The love he had seen every day was proof that they had really loved one another. But why did she have to sleep with him while she was still married to someone else? He could live with the fact that his father had been a murderer but, his mother an adulterer? No, he could not live with that.

He could never go home. He would rent a room and give up his studies. But then he would never get a decent job. These thoughts went round and round in his head for some time but at last he began to think rationally. His mother had said that she was very young when she married. He could accept that the marriage had been a mistake. She had also said that she and William had been friends for a long time. So, what if he had wormed his way into her affection and persuaded her to have an affair. After all she was only a woman and could be easily led.

He came up with a new scenario. Dad had seduced her – the Reid character had found out – Dad had killed him to keep him quiet and Mum had given him an alibi.

Yes, he could live with that.

He had been so engrossed in his research that he had not eaten all day. Now he was cold, hungry and it was getting dark. Mum would be getting worried. He would have to go home. He would have to close his mind to all he had found out and act as if nothing had happened.

'Hello Darling, you are home late. I was just beginning to worry.'

'Hi, Mum. Sorry. Was working on a project and forgot the time.'

'A project... sounds interesting. What is it about?'

'Nothing you'd be interested in. Is tea ready?'

'Yes. I'll serve it while you go and wash up.'

He never wants to share things with me, May thought wistfully, as her son pushed past her. It was different with William. He always had time to speak with me, no matter how tired he was. I miss those little talks we used to have while he was changing but I suppose you can't expect the same from a son. But why should he think I would not be interested in what he is doing? Or does he think I'm too stupid to understand?

Robert finished his tea and then excused himself saying he had homework to do. That at least was true. He had been so confused that he had missed whole nights of study and would have to catch up. Now that he had a plan it was all the more important that he succeed.

He would get good marks, go to Uni. He had enough saved up for that. Then, as soon as he was qualified, he would take his mother away from Brisbane where people still hadn't forgotten her past and he could give her a better life somewhere where no one knew her.

May had never felt so lonely. Though she believed he still loved her, Robert immersed himself in study. She would wait all day for his return but, apart from brief conversation during tea, he would take himself into his room to study. She tried to discuss his daily happenings, the subjects he was doing, his dreams for the future, but he had little to say in return.

It is like speaking to a statue, she thought. We seem to have nothing to say to each other. If only he would tell me what he is thinking. She became so worried about their strained relations that she began to get over her own outing.

Though the fashion business was no more, Elena and Angelina had continued dressmaking. More for company than interest May began dropping in and helped   when nobody was around. Soon her enthusiasm returned but she could not bring herself to begin designing again. Instead she turned her attention to developing Angelina's talent. It was with her encouragement that *Angelina* was born.

'Robert, your boy. He is always at his books,' Elena remarked one day. 'What's he going to be, Doctor?'

'I don't know Elena. He seems to have an aim but he does not discuss it with me.'

'He's good boy, May. Stays at home, studies. He'll get ahead. Not like my wild ones. We come here for a better life, but would they study? No. Left school as soon as they could, got shit jobs, spend all their money and run around with criminals. We might as well have stayed in Valetta. But my Angelina, she is my blessing. She is good girl. Does what her mother says. She will make a good mother one day.'

'She will also make a great fashion designer. She is so talented,' May agreed.

Angelina sat quietly listening to the two women discussing her as if she was not present. She didn't mind. She knew her mother loved her best of all her children and she would always be grateful to May for teaching her about fashion and design. Because of that she would be able to earn her own living. She would not be dependent on any man and she would only marry when she met a man who really loved her and was willing for her to pursue her own career. Or perhaps she would become a happy, independent old maid travelling to New York, London and Paris to worship at the temples of fashion.

CHAPTER 42

While still holding down a full-time job, Robert did so well in his final exams that he gained a scholarship to Queensland University. He was three months off eighteen when he began a Batchelor of Building Design Degree. May believed that it was because of William's influence that he chose the course but Robert explained,

'It's only a two year course so I will be able to start earning money in a couple of years and when I turn twenty-one I will be getting a good adult wage and you can become a lady of leisure,' he informed her.

Robert did not realize it, but his had been a very sheltered life. While he worked and studied, a revolution was going on in the real world. A generation of young people were growing up free from the worries of unemployment or war. They were better educated than their parents, had the opportunity to find work in almost any field they chose and, once working, were usually able to keep the money they earned. They began to question the traditions and values of their parents. And it was in universities that this movement was strongest.

Robert had imagined a university where the serious minded went to obtain degrees that would be their entry into a profession and a better life. Instead he found young men and women ready to take on the 'establishment.' They despised authority, material values and fidelity. Instead, they were for anti-poverty, anti-war and anti-censorship. Speeches and protests were the order of the day. It seemed to him that some spent their whole university years protesting.

Robert had had little interest in the opposite sex. When young he always thought that when he grew up he would marry Angelina. When he was about ten he realised that she was already a woman. Since then he had been too busy working and studying to find someone to take her place. Now he was surrounded by athletic, scantily clad, young women who did not regard marriage as a pre-requisite for sex. It was all very confusing and he had great difficulty in concentrating on his studies.

He was in the second year of his course when compulsory National Service was introduced for twenty-year old men. It meant that if one's name came up in the "Birthday Ballot," a non-discriminatory way of choosing recruits, one would be expected to serve two years in the regular army.

A year later, just as he was looking forward to a reward for all his years of study, his name came up in the lottery draw. He had not taken too much interest in the goings on in Indochina until he went to university. Like everyone else he had seen the graphic pictures of the self-immolation of Thich Quong Duc, but he knew nothing about the country or its politics. But on campus the name *Vietnam* seemed to be on everyone's lips. He attended several rallies and, though he did not see himself as a pacifist, he felt that Australia had no business being in this war. Now he was expected to be a part of it.

He discussed his options with a friend, Tom, a medical student who had three more years of study ahead of him and so was safe.

'What can I do, Tom? I'm not afraid of going. I just don't believe that we should be involved in this war.'

'You have three options, mate. You can go and fight in a war you do not believe in. You can refuse and be sent to jail. You can leave the country or hide and hope you don't get caught.'

"Well, the third's out. I can't leave Australia and I don't want to spend my life hiding my identity. There's been enough of that in my family already.'

'Then its Vietnam or jail. Is it war in general you object to or just this one?'

'I would have said that I believe in a just war, but who can say what that is? I'm anti-communist but I don't want to kill people over it. I think I'm against killing altogether really.'

'Then, my friend, I have the solution for you. You can become a soldier but as a conscientious objector you will be assigned to non-combatant duties.'

'How do I do that?'

'Well, you write a letter explaining your objections to killing. Have you ever belonged to the Quakers or something like that?'

'No, but I have always had great respect for them.'

'O.K. Then you must write a letter explaining clearly how you are against killing but that you are willing to serve in a non-combat role, get a couple of character references from a few important people, I can help you with that, then send it along with your registration.'

'What will happen then?'

'You will probably be called to an interview where you will have to argue your case.'

'What is non-combat duty?'

'Anything that does not involved actual front line action, cooks, porters, drivers, all kinds of things. Hey, I've just had an idea. How do you feel about blood and gore and dying people?'

'I don't know. Never had to face anything like that. But I'm not squeamish if that's what you mean.'

'Then what about becoming a medic?'

'A medic ... yes, I could do that.'

'Well, while you are waiting for your call up, enrol in an advanced first aid course, St. Johns do a great one, then you will have something to bargain with.'

'Yes, I could do that. Thanks Tom. I'll get on to it straight away.'

Robert went to Vietnam and though he never fired a shot in anger he often experienced being fired on as he was helicoptered in and out, retrieving the wounded. It was during those years that he grew to manhood and realised how narrow his upbringing had been. Once he had seen the world in black and white. Now he knew that there were many shades of grey and many ways to tell a story. His medical training had given him compassion, his mixing with diverse men and women taught him that there was good and bad in everybody and his first-hand experience of war made him a dedicated pacifist. He vowed he would spend the rest of his life doing what he could to make life easier for the marginalised and outcasts.

Robert was proud of the work he had done and the men he had

served with. He was bewildered by the reception they encountered when they returned to Australia. They were insulted, vilified, treated like pariahs.

He believed, like many people, that Australia had made a mistake in entering the war in the first place, and the outcome had been a disaster. But to pillory the men who had been sent, mostly against their will, to fight, was a disgrace. He argued with his pacifist friends but they were so committed to their cause that they would not listen.

'It was not our choice to go,' he argued. 'The government sent us. Anyway most of us weren't even regular army. We were just the unlucky ones whose names came up.'

'You could have refused to go.'

'And be sent to gaol?'

'Better than marching into another country and killing innocent people.'

'I didn't kill people. I was a medic.'

'But you went so that's just as bad.'

There was no arguing with them and he wasn't sure he wanted to. They were so ignorant of real life. From their privileged state as pampered students in the luckiest country on earth, what did they know about the sufferings of people in third world countries or the wonderful fellowships of servicemen? He felt himself an adult amid a group of spoilt children.

In disgust Robert decided to restart his life in another state where no one had known him as the rather supercilious child he had been. He begged May to come with him but she could not imagine living anywhere but Brisbane. It may have treated her badly at times but she loved the city, she loved its people and most of all she had found her home with the Bazzinas.

Robert moved to Adelaide and, with the aid of free university fees granted by the Whitlam government, he enrolled at Adelaide University to begin a Bachelor of Science in Public Health and devoted the rest of his life to making the world a better place for all mankind.

When the next group of migrants, now called Boat People, began arriving he did all he could to help them become citizens.

'If it was good enough for Australia to send young men to fight and die for these people I cannot think of a reason why we can't welcome them into our country when they are no longer safe in their own,' he told anyone who would listen.

He married an Adelaide girl he met at university and together they had one child, a boy. They named him Stephen after St Stephen, the first martyr who had been willing to die rather than deny his God. Robert hoped that it would be an inspiration for his son.

CHAPTER 43

ADELAIDE 2008

There really is a God.

Yesterday a letter arrived, addressed to my grandmother, which may change the course of my life, or at least make it a little easier. Until now I had managed to forestall any enquiries about my proposed partner. I was getting pretty good at changing the conversation long before it got to a sensitive subject. But just when I thought I would have to defy Grandmother and bring on a family disaster, the wonderful letter arrived.

The envelope was of superior quality. I had picked up the mail, as it was Saturday, and turned it over and over as I drove back from the post office. I even contemplated steaming it open, but that was really only a though. Instead I made sure I was there when it was opened.

Inside, on luxurious paper, with a very fancy crest, was a letter from a pioneer historic society. It was an invitation, for Flora Jean Henderson-Mudge, to attend a weekend of speeches and celebration during which the historic mansion, *Inverrigan* was to be officially handed over to the historic society to become a museum, dedicated to the history of the pastoral industry in Queensland.

There was a flurry of '*goodness mes*' and '*how surprisings*' and, for once, dear Grandmother lost her cool. She had to sit down and read the letter several times before she could quite take it in and tell us its contents. Mother was fluttering around, almost as excited. It took a calm, disinterested person like me to bring them to their senses.

'Grandmother, isn't *Inverrigan* your old home?'

'Yes it is, my dear.' She was truly beaming. 'It is the home that your Great- great–grandfather built for his Jeannie when they retired to Brisbane. It is the house where I was born.'

'But didn't the "dastardly relatives" do you out of it?'

'The dastardly relatives? Oh, you mean Charles and his family? **Them.** They sold it years ago. It was a private hospital for many years I believe. I'm afraid my cousins had no sense of history. Can you imagine a mansion like that being turned into a hospital? Of course they had no appreciation of history, no understanding of the sacrifices their forbears had made to give them the life they have. They sold it without a second thought. The last I heard, it was sadly neglected. It's a wonder it has escaped the destruction of development.'

'And you are going to go to this celebration?' I crossed my fingers hoping that family pride would override her loathing of Charles and his family.

'Of course I am. I am the oldest living representative of the Hendersons of *Inverrigan*. I will be proud to represent my forbears. I can think of no finer future for my old home than as a museum for those who pioneered the sheep industry in Queensland. It is only just that they should be honoured.

'We must all go. Perhaps you could take a few days off from school, Sally, and join me. It is time that you should come to know a little of those who sacrificed so much to give you the life you have.'

I was a bit lukewarm about spending time with her but I thought this might give me a chance to further my investigation about the rumoured murder, but when I looked, the date clashed with the formal.

'Grandmother, I'd love to go but it's the same weekend as the formal. I can't really miss that, can I?'

'Oh dear no, I do not think you can.' Suddenly all the joy disappeared. 'So that means your mother will not be able to travel with me either.' All the sparkle faded from her eyes. 'Perhaps I will not go after all.'

This was the first Mum had heard about her going to Brisbane. She wasn't very pleased. Time with her mother and a whole bag of history buffs was not her idea of a holiday. 'No, Mother, you must go. It is important for the family name. Perhaps a friend, Mrs Drummond, perhaps, could go with you. You enjoy her company.'

Trust my mum to come up with an acceptable solution. Most times she behaves as if she is willing to go along with any of grandmother's wishes, but when it doesn't suit her she always seems to come up with an idea to save the day.

The joy was back again. 'Yes, Laura. We have been talking of taking another trip ever since we went on that little cruise last year. We could even go to one of those luxury island hideaways afterwards. I will have to ring her later and see if she is interested. But it would mean I would miss your special evening, Sally.'

I could see she wasn't all that disappointed. A formal didn't stand a chance beside the celebration of the Henderson legend, or pampered luxury in an exclusive retreat.

'Grandmother, you've already planned everything and I know you don't really enjoy a horde of young people. I'll be so sorry you won't be there but we'll take loads of pictures. The Formal hardly compares with something like this. It's not like as if it's a wedding or something. You owe it to the family to attend.'

'You're right, of course. I hope you are not disappointed.' Grandmother gave me a sad smile, but I could see she was pleased.

'I'll survive,' I muttered then turned away before she could see the glee in my eyes.

Later in the day I was looking through the travel supplement of the Saturday Advertiser. I read it from cover to cover every week, dreaming of escaping from my life at *Glencoe.* And there was another miracle.

'Grandmother.' In my excitement I raised my voice, which earned a frown from Flora Henderson-Mudge. I apologised. 'I didn't mean to raise my voice, Grandmother but this is really exciting. It's as if fate is smoothing your way to Brisbane.'

''Do not be ridiculous, Sally. There is no such thing as fate. Everyone creates their own destiny.'

'You're probably right, but this is certainly a co-incidence,' and I showed her the article. 'There is a cruise ship leaving Melbourne going to Hobart, Sydney, Brisbane and Cairns and the timing is perfect. It docks in Brisbane on the same Friday of the weekend celebrations. You and Mrs Drummond could fly to Melbourne, cruise to Brisbane, go to the opening and then, either fly home, re-join the cruise or extend your journey to stay at the Whit Sundays or somewhere like that.'

She took the article from me. If it were anyone else I would have said 'grabbed,' but Flora Hamilton-Mudge would never do anything so unladylike, but it certainly went from my hand to hers faster than the speed of light.

The gleam was back in her eye. 'Sally, how clever of you. I will ring Laura now. I do hope she is free. She is such good company. Cruising is a wonderful way to travel but one cannot always rely on the conversation of strangers.' She went to her own sitting room to ring her friend, looking very pleased with herself.

And I was more than pleased too. Now I could have Joel as my partner without upsetting anybody. Suddenly the world was becoming a wonderful place.

'Thank you, God,' I whispered.

CHAPTER 44

The evening, it went off like a song. My dress was a complete success. It was an Angelina original, turquoise silk, with an off the shoulder, sweetheart bodice and a full, flowing skirt. It made me look almost feminine. The colour reminded me of the sea so I imagined myself a mermaid. My hair is a mousy brown but that night, with the help of colour and extensions I could almost see myself in a Disney movie.

My best friend Lucy, to honour her heritage chose a modified Chan Sam. She has the figure and the grace to wear something like that. Marcia's dress was a cloud of soft pink organza. She seemed to float. I had never imagined that three blue stockings like us could look so glamorous.

We were picked up in a stretch limousine arranged by our dates. We thought they were very sophisticated until we found that half the other girls came in similar transportation. It's the latest thing, so we were informed.

We had all been pretending that a formal was no big thing, but secretly we were enjoying the chance to be celebrities, if only for one night. It takes a lot for a girl to feel special these days.

We all admired each other's dresses, and thankfully nobody's choice had been replicated. It would be an absolute disaster if someone else turned up in the same dress when our parents had gone to so much expense. There are stories of that happening some years.

Of course Cherelle Myres had pushed the bounds of respectability to the limit, scarlet taffeta, back down to the crack and cleavage that left nothing to the imagination, but she was trying to prove a point. She had always been a rebel. It was only her pedigree and the chance that she might bring glory to the dear old school with her brilliant exam results that had saved her from expulsion many times. This was her last act of defiance. She no longer had to abide by Alexandra Ladies Academy standards. Short of barring her way, the powers that be could not stop her being part of the proceedings.

We, less brave, were proud of her. All we hoped was that the wires and the glue that held the dress up would not fail her when the real dancing began. It is one thing to glide around in a sedate waltz but another thing altogether to throw one's self into hip-hop or Latin tango.

The function was over by eleven, giving us time to celebrate in our own way. Some went home the way they came, but others got taxis or walked with their guys to Hindley Street or, like Joel and me, to secluded spots for a little, quiet romancing.

Joel had already selected a spot along the Torrens. A little green monster inside me wondered who else he had brought there before me. We were suddenly quite shy. We spoke of everyday things, both unsure where this would lead. This was the first really serious snogging I had ever been engaged in and I didn't know the rules. I had a secret feeling that Joel was pretty much in the same boat as me. Neither of us had read the handbook.

There was a little pecking and fumbling, a bit of hesitant exploration, during which Joel happened to touch my ribs. How was he to know that I am the most easily tickled person in the world? I let out a loud shriek that must have frightened him to death and then burst into laughter.

It was the library all over again.

After that, all the silly pre-courting rituals seemed crass. We lay back on the grass held hands and began to speak like real people, telling each other of our hopes and aspirations, our ambitions and our fears. The stupid family business was not mentioned. We were just two people who liked each other, getting to know a little more about one another.

Joel was most amused when I told him about my plan to escape Glencoe by way of university.

'But when you find this distant university what do you really want to do there?

'I haven't got a clue really. Just getting away has been my ambition as long as I can remember.'

'Uni isn't a destination you know. It's a place where you earn your ticket to the future.'

'My, aren't you the one. You should go into advertising, writing slogans. You could make a fortune.'

'And can I use you as a reference? No, I'm not a P.A. guy. I'm a builder. I want to make things, design houses, construct bridges, that sort of thing.'

'It must be great to know what you want to do. Me, the only thing I've ever been passionate about is travel. I want to see the world.'

'Then you should join the Navy.'

'Ha, ha. No thanks. I've had enough of following rules. I know I've got to fill in my applications in the next few days but I still haven't any strong feeling about anything except getting away.'

'Perhaps you could become a foreign correspondent then.'

'I don't think there's a special course for that but it's a thought. Perhaps journalism will be my way out. Grandmother Flora will probably have a fit, hardly a profession for a Henderson, but who cares. At least I'll be going to university, and one as far from here as possible.'

Joel laughed. 'Me. I'll be happy with good old Adelaide Uni. That is unless I become such a star that some footy club picks me in the draft.'

I was impressed. 'Are you really that good?'

'In my dreams but, talking of football, I have a game tomorrow, so Cinderella, I had better take you home before you turn into a pumpkin.'

Of course that set us off on another bout of laughter. It we were as funny to the world as we were to each other we could make a fortune as comedians.

When we got home the light was on and Mum was waiting for us in her dressing gown.

'Safe home,' she said. 'You both looked beautiful. I thought you were the smartest couple on the floor. Did you have a good time after?' She had a special gleam in her eye. Ever the romantic, I think she would have been happy if we announced our nuptials then and there.

I raised my eyebrows 'Yes, Mother. We talked and talked until we knew everything about each other and we've vowed eternal friendship for the rest of our lives.' I grinned at Joel and he gave me a little, brotherly squeeze.

'Then would you like to stay for a coffee?' she asked Joel.

'Thanks, but no. I must go. I promised coach I'd be home by midnight. He'd cut me from tomorrow's game if he knew I was out so late.'

'Then how about dinner on Sunday?'

'Do you mean dinner at twelve or proper "dinner", at seven?'

We all laughed. 'Six thirty for seven if it suits you.'

Joel shook hands with Mum, gave me a peck on the cheek and left. As we walked inside Mum gave me a hug. 'I really do like that boy. Isn't it lucky that Mother is away?'

I was happy with the peck on the cheek. I wanted to think a bit more about our relationship. Perhaps the reason why I had blown it up into a big romance was because he was the first real live guy I had ever had any feelings for. Up to now all my dreamboats were in posters on my wall.

Maybe this crazy feeling was no more than friendship?

CHAPTER 45

He rang me, on Sunday, and told me that yes, his team had won but no, he had not got a Rising Star award so he might still have to rely on his brains to provide a future.

'Sal, I was helping Dad clean out a few things in the garage this morning when I found a suitcase that used to belong to Grandpa. It seems to be full of papers and things. Dad said he was always going to look through it but never found the time. I offered to give up some of my precious study time to do it for him. That pleased him. So, as soon as I hang up, I am going to tip the whole lot onto my bedroom floor and go through it. Maybe I'll find the answer to the family mystery but don't get your hopes up. I'll tell you all about it when I come for "dinner".'

I couldn't wait. I had planned to do some study too but I couldn't concentrate. This new life is ruining my well-trained brain. What with my mixed feelings for Joel and my trying to guess the family mystery I'm starting to worry that, not only would I not get the wonderful marks I wanted, but that I would fail altogether and have to repeat.

Just imagine, a granddaughter of Flora Henderson Mudge failing an exam!!!

As soon as Joel arrived that evening I whispered, 'Any joy?'

'Yeah. Tell you later.'

The evening was warm. Perhaps spring has finally decided to stay around for a while. Mum had prepared a salad with the regulation roast and a scrumptious pav. for sweets. We three sat around the smaller table in the sunroom and chatted about everyday things, the state of the nation, the latest movies and of course the football, which was now reaching its annual crises of finals. We each had our teams and boasted about, or commiserated on, their chances of reaching them.

What will pass for general conversation when the football season is over, I wonder? Oh, of course cricket, but there will be no divergence of opinion there. After all, we're all Aussies.

Mum declined Joel's offer to help with the dishes and left us to continue our conversation, informing us that she just had to watch Bed of Roses, a hint that we would not be disturbed. She was giving the romance, if there was one, every chance.

She was hardly out the door when I demanded, 'What did you find?'

Joel could feel my excitement but wanted to tell it his own way. 'There was lots of uninteresting stuff. The odd letter or two, bills, bank statements, investment advice, you know.

'There were a few photos, not as many as I hoped and, of course, no names or dates written on the back, but there are one or two of a woman and a small boy. I'm surmising that they are of Grandpa and his mum but,' here he paused to give his announcement the dramatic tension it deserved, 'there was this,' and with that he produced an envelope and proceeded to pull out a couple of pages of writing paper.

'I'm not going to give you a summary. You can read it all yourself and then we'll talk about the contents.'

I was so excited my hands trembled as I opened it. The paper was thin and the writing a bit spidery but easy to read.

Dear Robert, it began, *I am very happy that you are doing so well. Thank you for your letter and your concern for me. It was good of you to again suggest it but I do not wish to relocate. I am being well cared for here. Brisbane has always been my home and I wish to die here and be buried beside my darling Willie. It grieves me that you are still angry with your father and believe that he had given me an unhappy life. Nothing could be further from the truth. Willie and I loved each other and every day spent with him was one of joy. My only regret is that it was so short. Still he is with me, every day, in spirit.*

I must now correct a belief, which I know you have had for many years and, to my shame, I have never had the courage to change. When I told you, those many years ago, that you must never mention the reason for that fight you had at school as it would upset your father, it was not that he was guilty of the crime, but that the memory of it would cause him pain. Also, I was too much of a coward to tell you the true story. But I must put my own feelings behind me and do what I can, at this late date, to clear my poor Willie's name. It is not only an old but a long story. However I will try to tell it as precisely and as truthfully as I can.

You know my maiden name was Swann, but what you didn't know was that I was, for several years, Mrs May Henderson, the wife of an important member of Brisbane society. That big house that we used to go and look at when you were little had been my home for most of my life, not through birth, but through the good will of Douglas Henderson. When I was of age, he married me. There was a great disparity in ages but I think he really did love me and I had feelings for him too. Before we married Willie had been my best friend. He loved me and I had toyed with his affections, but I was young then and did not understand real love.

One of the reasons Douglas married me was to produce an heir, but though he did not know it, he was infertile. So to satisfy his wish and, I must confess, to secure my future, I enticed Willie into a relationship, which resulted in my daughter, Flora.

Here I couldn't help looking up at Joel and saying 'that means'.

'Yes,' he nodded, 'but read on. There's more.'

Douglas never guessed. He truly loved Flora, but there was a matter of inheritance. He needed a son. So about four years later I decided to try again and to my shame again enticed poor Willie. But this time my secret was discovered by a horrible man called Gerard Reid.

This next part is hard to write, my dear son, but you must only remember that I was young, foolish and selfish. I had been brought up to think that the world revolved around me.

I was in our summerhouse one evening when this odious man arrived, told me he had proof of my infidelity and demanded that I give him sex for his silence.

I was horrified by the suggestion and pushed him away as he came towards me. He fell, hitting his head and died. I was terrified. I knew that no one would believe it was an accident and in those days the punishment would have been death.

In my panic I called your father and begged him to dispose of the body. Wonderful man that he was, he agreed for my sake, but unfortunately the car, with Gerard in it, did not go over the cliff as it was supposed to.

His death was declared a crime and by a series of mishaps Willie became a suspect and was put on trial for murder. He could have immediately cleared his name by telling the truth but he would not betray me. Can you imagine? He was willing to be found guilty and hanged rather than reveal my name. I couldn't let him do it so, on the last day of the trial, I lied under oath and told the judge that he had been with me all night so could not have killed Gerard or disposed of his body. Thank God my story was believed. Willie was freed, but because Douglas was such an important man it was a national scandal. We were pariahs. Willie lost his well-paid job and we had to live a life of shame in South Brisbane.

Robert, you must understand that though we bore the scorn of society, we were the happiest couple in Brisbane. I had found true love and your father loved me till the day he died. He loved you too Robert, but you always pushed him away. I didn't help. Having lost a daughter I think I loved you selfishly. I didn't want to share you with anyone, not even your father.

Please forgive me and know that your father loved you. Do not think evil of him. Think only that he was a noble man who never hurt anyone in his life.

I am much too unwell to come south to you. My time is nearly done. I only hope you can still love me after you have read this. Just know that you were loved by Willie and by me from the moment you were born.

Your Mother, May Swann.

Have you ever seen a rubber tyre get a puncture and slowly collapse as the air seeps out? Well, that is how I felt. The shock about Flora and then Robert was bad enough, but the rest of it! It was too much to take in at one reading. I could hear myself saying, 'Nos... I don't believe this ... and O My Gods' ... but it took several minutes for the full implication of what I was reading to sink in. Not only were Joel and I relater through both our great grandparents, but our Great Grandmother had killed someone and our Great Grandfather had been willing to take the blame and die for her! If I had read it in a book I would have found it hard to believe, but here was the proof, written in her own hands by my G.G.M. May Swann!

'Well,' I finally managed to blurt out. 'We sure are the product of two very unusual people.'

'That's what I thought. How much of them is in us, do you think? I'm afraid, Sal, that if you knock someone off, I'm not going to take the wrap for you.'

'Not very gallant, Cuz, but ditto for me. Though it is very romantic. He must have been a special person.'

'Or a sucker for punishment. She uses him twice to procreate, then dumps a murder on him. I call that way beyond the call of duty.'

'But a real hero. He must have really loved her.'

Joel's expression became serious. 'Sal, you know this kissing cousin business. We ought to think that over a bit, don't you think?' He sounded quite embarrassed.

'Don't worry. I had already changed my mind about that even before I read this letter.'

'What, dumping me already?' He looked relieved.

'No, not dumping, just re-evaluating the situation. I've comforted too many of my friends not to know where first romances go. First the great love affair then the big bust up. I like you too much for that. I want you as a friend that I can keep. Ever since Grampy-Mudge died I've wanted a big brother. We've got lots of the same blood, so we are sort of related anyway.'

I wanted to make him realise that I wasn't just rattling on. I wanted him to see that I was serious so I stood and looked him in the eye. 'Joel, will you be my big brother?'

He gave a little, embarrassed laugh. ,'Hey, this is getting serious,' then realising what I had asked, he sobered up. 'Sal, you realise what you are asking? Do you really mean it?'

'Yes, I do.'

'Being a brother is not just an on and off thing you know. If I agree we will be attached to each other for the rest of our lives, in bad times as well as good.'

'That's what I want. To know someone is on my side at all times.'

'Being on your side doesn't mean that I'll always agree with you. If I'm your big brother it will be my duty to sometimes tell you what you don't want to hear.'

'Grandmother has been doing that all my life.'

'Yes, but I'll expect you to take me seriously. What if I questioned your choice of boyfriend for instance?'

'I'd take your objections seriously because I would know you were doing it for my own good, not just to uphold tradition.'

'But would you do as I say?'

'Depends on your objections. But I would take them seriously. And, as your sister, I will have the same privileges.'

'Then my answer is yes. Should we have a little ceremony or something?'

'Let's just hold hands and promise to always be there for each other.'

And that's just what we did. Afterwards we both burst into laughter again, but that didn't mean that we weren't serious about our promise.

'Joel,' I said, when we were in control again, 'what are we

going to do about the information in the letter. Should we tell anyone?'

'Who, for instance?'

'Well, perhaps your dad and my mum, not Grandmother though.

'Why not? She's the only one who really needs to know. It won't make any difference to the other two.'

'No. We can't tell dear old Flora. It would kill her.'

'Then, that's your answer. It's either everybody or no one. I'm afraid, Little Sister, we will have to take our secret to the grave.'

'But what am I going to tell Mum? She's already hearing wedding bells for us.'

'Just tell her that you like me too much to ruin it by marrying me.'

I really like my Big Brother.

CHAPTER 46

Next morning, while I was munching away at my toast, the telephone rang. I wasn't expecting a call but listened as Mum answered it.

'Goodness! What happened?

'What is wrong with her? Is she still in hospital?

I stood up and went to her side. 'What's happened Mum?'

'Shh. Mother's collapsed.' Then to the voice on the phone. 'She's flying home? When? ... Oh dear, all right I'll be there... 'Yes Virgin 2.50. . . No I don't need the number of the flight. I'll be there. Tell her not to worry. I'll be there.' And she put down the phone.

'Mum, is it grandmother? Is she all right?'

Mum needed a nearby chair. 'Give me a minute, Sally. Could you pour me a cuppa and I'll tell you.'

I was unused to seeing my mother in a flap. I could see that she was shocked. It had something to do with Grandmother. I poured her a cuppa and waited. She took a sip and then sat back and explained.

'That was Laura Drummond. It appears that yesterday your grandmother collapsed and someone called an ambulance. She had recovered before she got to the hospital, insisted that there was nothing wrong with her, but they kept her in, just in case. Of course she was furious so they discharged her first thing this morning but she wants to come straight home. Mrs Drummond has booked her on the first flight she could get. Mother insists on flying alone. She forbad Laura from changing her own holiday plans. There was nothing wrong with her, she insisted. She just wanted to come home, immediately.

'Laura said it was easier to agree than argue. I can understand that. But she is going to cut her trip short and will be home in a few days. She would rather they had flown home together but, of course, Mother wouldn't hear of it. But it means that she will be flying in on her own, today, so I will have to be there to meet her.'

I have rarely seen my mother lose her cool but this time she was flapping around like a fly who'd just been sprayed. I could see that my calming presence was needed but I was secretly panicking too. What had grandmother discovered?

'But why did she collapse? Did she have a heart attack or something?'

'No. There doesn't seem to be anything seriously wrong with her. Mrs Drummond said that they were having a great time. Mother was looking at some old memorabilia when she suddenly stood up, then fainted. The doctor who examined her said that she was in overall good health but her symptoms were like those of someone who had had a shock. He thought all the excitement might have been too much for her.'

'I doubt that. She usually loves being the centre of attention.'

Then a dreadful thought came to me. She was looking at old history. She's found out about May, and the murder? Even worse, she might have found out about her origin. Should I tell Mum and prepare her for the worst? No, that might create more problems. I will have to get to Grandmother first and find out what actually happened. I will have to be there when she arrived. Being the custodian of the family secret was getting more complicated by the minute.

'Mum, I know how you hate parking at the Airport. Why don't I drop you off then park the car while you go into the terminal and wait for her?'

'You can't Sal. You have got school.'

'Sooo, my entire education career is going to go down the tube if I miss one day? Don't worry, I'll ring the school and give them a good excuse,'

'Don't tell a lie. Don't say you're sick.' Mum is very suspicious. She thinks that if you tell lies they might come true.

'Don't worry Mum. I'll just tell them we have a family crisis.'

'Sally!'

'Well, it's the truth. Something terrible must have happened to get Flora Henderson to faint. It's so unladylike.'

I skipped school that day and drove Mum to the airport instead. There were no major dramas on the way and we were in good time to meet the plane. From what I could see Grandmother seemed to be holding up very well. However she didn't comment that I was here on a school day, so something must be wrong. Perhaps her formidable reserve was wearing thin.

Apart from an assurance that she was "quite well, thank you" she was silent on the trip home but as soon as we were inside the house she seemed to collapse into herself, her face turned deathly white and, for once, she looked all of her sixty-seven years.

'Mother, are you O.K.? Do you want to lie down? Should I call the doctor?'

'Lavinia, stop fussing. Just let me sit for a while. Perhaps you could pour me a small brandy.'

She did. Grandmother took a couple of sips then, as the colour returned to her cheeks, she began her explanation.

'Sit down, both of you. I think I owe you both an explanation. I will tell you exactly what happened. I still feel embarrassed about fainting. I have never done anything like that before. But there were mitigating circumstances.'

She's found out, I thought. She's found out about the scandal, but does she know it all? I could see that she was gathering all her strength to go on with her story.

'The celebrations on Saturday went off well. Several important gentlemen made speeches. I have the program with me. You can read it later. They have done a wonderful job restoring the house and there are rooms where people can go to study the history of the sheep industry as well as amazing memorabilia, paintings and diaries of early pioneers. I could have spent a month there.

'I also met several old school and family friends. One of my cousins, Stewart, was there, a very old man now, but I could see my father in him. His family invited us to a late lunch next day. Afterwards one of my grandnieces brought out some old family albums hoping I could identify the people in them.

'Among the photos was one taken at Father's wedding. Do you know that was the first time I had ever seen my mother's face. I was very moved. She was so young and very beautiful. No wonder my father loved her. And then there was one of the whole family and. . .'

Here she stopped and took another sip to give her the courage to go on. I was holding my breath dreading what would come next.

'There was one of the whole family, my father and mother, Uncle Charles and his wife and the two boys. But there was one more person there. I looked closely and realised who she was.

'That's Jess,' I said 'Why is she in the family photo? ... and then, oh Lavinia, I can still hardly believe it ...' Stewart said, "Why shouldn't she be there? After all she was your grandmother."

She lost it then. Put her head in her hands and cried. No, crying is too weak a word for it. She howled. Flora Henderson-Mudge lost her cool and howled like a banshee. Mother and I stood there, not knowing what to do. Not knowing how to console her.

Eventually she regained her composure. She raised her head and looked at us with so much pain in her eyes that I nearly started crying myself.

'Jess was my Grandmother. All my life I had thought of her as a family servant. She cared for me all those years and I treated her with contempt. When I left Queensland I didn't even ask her to come with me. I just abandoned her. I think I sent her one Christmas card but after that she was just someone who had been around in my former life. I didn't give her another thought, and she was my grandmother!'

Tears formed in her eyes and ran down her cheeks but this time she kept her cool. She wiped them away with a small handkerchief then turned towards me and took my hand

'She was my grandmother, just as I am yours, Sally. Can you imagine living in this house with me and regarding me as a servant?'

'I could never do that,' I assured her and I meant it.

'I know dear, but could you imagine it. I don't mean that I was ever horrid to her or anything, but I had no great regard for her. She had been a mother to me all those years, sacrificed her own life so that she could always be there when I needed her and I never knew that she was my grandmother.'

I could imagine how it felt. Flora Henderson-Mudge might have been the bane of my existence but she loved me and, hand on heart, I loved her too. I didn't know what to say. We do not do emotions in our house but I squeezed her hand and she responded.

'Mother, it was not your fault,' Mum said. 'Maybe she never mentioned it to save your father's feelings, or perhaps they thought you already knew. She obviously loved you very much so just being there to care for you must have given her great joy. I will write to the relatives and ask them to send a copy of the wedding photo. Then the family will be complete.'

Trust my mum to say the right thing.

The picture of Douglas Henderson still dominates the reception room but on the mantel in the lounge room is a large wedding photo of all the family at the wedding. In grandmother's sitting room is a smaller one of Jess, and one of May, taken from it. Grandmother dusts them each day and often there are tears in her eyes.

I know now that Joel was right. The scandal is yesterday's business. All those involved are long since dead. Talking about it now would change nothing and only hurt Grandmother.

We will have to take our secret to the grave, but the writer in me can't help thinking it would make a great story.

CHAPTER 46

BRISBANE - 1973

Two a.m. and all was peaceful in the little room. The staff, half-jokingly, called it the *waiting room* for it was there that a resident, nearing death, was taken. If they had relatives, this was where they sat waiting out the last few hours, in private, with their loved one. It was where the religious had their final anointing. It was where tears were shed and thanks given for a life lived, as it embarked on its last journey.

The room was in darkness except for a soft glow coming from the night-lights in the passage.

Ellen, after another routine check was stepping quietly into the passage just as Teresa passed.

'Is it over?' she whispered

'No, but it won't be long. Is there anybody who should be notified?' Ellen spoke softly out of respect for the dying woman.

'No. She has no relatives. She used to be a nurse, you know before she came to live here.'

'Should we call a minister or a priest?'

'No. She doesn't seem to have had any religious affiliation. But I couldn't imagine her ever doing anything bad. She was a real angel. Everybody here loved her. If she doesn't get into heaven there's not much hope for the rest of us. She'd have nothing to confess.'

The door was still open and, though they spoke softly, Jessica could hear them. They thought she was beyond hearing but, though she could not respond, she still could hear.

Nothing to confess, she thought. If only they knew. She had tried to lead a good life but circumstances always seemed to get in the way. She had meant to be a good wife for Darby but the war had ruined that.

She had shared her body with Douglas because she loved him and believed he loved her too, but time had proved her wrong. Still, she had at least been faithful to him and had stayed with him to the end, even when she knew that he was ruined.

She had loved and protected Flora all her life but often wondered why she had let her go without telling her the truth about herself. Surely that wouldn't be held against her, if there were an accounting in the hereafter.

But May, had she done right by May? She had always loved her daughter but with a fearful love. Had it been for May's sake, or her own fear of being left destitute, that had made her persuade her daughter to marry Douglas?

And what about the rest? May would never have thought of encouraging William. That had been entirely her suggestion. She knew, in her heart of hearts, that Douglas would never have divorced May. He would have been disappointed, perhaps turned his attentions to another woman, but he would never have divorced her for, whatever else he was, he was an honourable man. It had been her own fear of losing position that had prompted that.

No, that was a crime, her sin to confess, and it had led to all the rest. And that too had been her crime. She had ruined the future for young William. She had done that for a selfish reason. For it had not been only hers and May's future that was at stake. It was Flora's, and she had, at least protected her.

Jessica had suspected the worst when she had steamed open the letter. Though it hinted rather than accused, the meaning was obvious. Gerard knew that William and May were lovers and he had been astute enough to link that fact to Flora's birth. She had always wondered why Douglas had believed the Chinese herb story so quickly, but he wanted an heir so badly. Even if he had had some doubt, his desire for an heir and wanting proof of his own fertility had made it an easy choice. The thought of having his failure made public would have driven him mad.

Perhaps he would not disown Flora, for he truly loved her, but even the risk was too much. She would have to talk to May straight away and they would have to come up with a plan to stop Gerard before he got to Douglas.

As she hurried down to the summerhouse she heard the scream. She ran the last few yards and threw open the door. May was standing, still screaming, staring at the floor. Gerard was lying, full stretch, on the floor and blood was running onto the tiles.

She felt a moment's satisfaction.

Good. He is dead.

Then the full implications sank in. Here was a crisis and she must deal with it.

'He came at me Mother. He came at me and wanted to rape me.'

Jessica took her daughter in her arms, turned her away from

the sight of the body, and looked into her eyes.

'Shh, shh, Darling. I know you did not mean it. But it is done.'

While she tried to calm her daughter her brain was desperately trying to think of a solution. Gerard was dead, unfortunate, but good news. The manner of his death would be a catastrophe if not handled properly. She needed help, but from whom? William's face came into her mind. He loved May and so far had kept her secret. Could he be trusted? She thought he could.

First, calm May, next call William then, come up with a good plan.

'May, you must calm down. Then go to the house and ring William, yes William. He is the one person we can trust ... Tell him you need him here, immediately. Tell him to get a taxi.'

But that would mean involving someone else. It probably didn't matter but best if no one knew that he was here.

'Tell him to get a taxi but to get out before he gets to this place and walk the rest of the way ...' While she was giving instructions a proper plan was forming in her mind.

May, relieved that someone else was taking charge, hurried off to do her mother's bidding.

Jessica began cleaning up the worst of the blood. If everything went to plan, the body would never be found, but she would wipe away anything that could link him to this place.

As she looked at the man who could have ruined all their lives, she thought she saw a slight movement in his neck. Was it a pulse? She placed her fingers on the spot and felt it, a slight one, but it was there. Their troubles weren't over. He wasn't dead after all.

She reached for the cushion.

Was it the only thing to do? Yes.

Was she sorry for what she had done? No.

They say a mother would do anything to protect her child. That was all she had done, protected her daughter and granddaughter.

She could never ask forgiveness for that because she could never say she was sorry.

The End

www.ingramcontent.com/pod-product-compliance
Lightning Source LLC
Chambersburg PA
CBHW072355110726
47909CB00003B/715